THE GAR DEN

ADVANCE PRAISE FOR THE GARDEN

The Garden [Director's Cut] is an amplified exposition of the original. In this complete version Louis Armand takes you into hyper-imaginative zones as astounding as a Moroccan garden - as seductive as its fragrance and as artfully designed. It's a chimerical tale of disorientation and lust - the chronicle of a writer with debilitated perception 'pouring His morose soul into His writing-machine'.

Pam Brown

Conceived «in the confrontation of light & intractable unlight», this incredible piece of the supreme Manichean and above all, post-Epicurean writing, sums up the best traditions of contemporary « Western » literary thinking and that Eastern one, exemplified by Nizami's Diwan or Attar of Nishapur's The Conference of the Birds. Above all, this « novel » or the author's travelogue breaths through the air and floats above the hot dunes of human history in the brightest daylight of contemporary fiction.

Nina Zivancevic

Imagine being on a movie set of a film modernizing the story of Marduk and Tiamat, with a script based on the writings of Georges Bataille and Maurice Blanchot, and the actor playing the Marduk character asks the director for his motivation in the scene when he first meets Tiamat, unaware that the director is on speed. The director riffs *The Garden*.

Gregory L. Ulmer

Louis Armand makes the exquisite corpses of yesterday look like tomorrow's spectacular dreams. His writing is a flare in the dark.

D. Harlan Wilson

The Garden Director's Cut is a short book (156 pages), a kind of novella inviting its reader to discover its one single unpunctuated sentence, and associates its enigmatic text with an explicit introduction and references to a trip to Morocco, to the *Book of Genesis*, Bosch's *Garden of Earthly Delights*, Shaykh Nefzawi's *Perfumed Garden*, Pierre Guyotat's *Eden Eden Eden*, and Derek Jarman's films.

The Garden does not make these references coalesce because it describes a constant state of Non-Being, which is to be associated with sparse images of Being and the expression of non-alienation. To evoke the state of Non-Being and non-alienation requires not a poetics of negativity but of fragmentation and continuity. The long and unpunctuated sentence shows a series of short semantic segments which are linked without any logic or actantial coherence and clear chain of action and are however cohesive.

The figures of two characters emerge, a woman M, who is dead, and a man; one voice is constantly present. These characters and this voice are fragments which unite, disunite and offer images of bodies, sufferings, and make it possible to evoke obvious Moroccan realities and their Muslim background.

Book of coalescences and undoubted realities, *The Garden* is a whole and does not let imagine any totality; it is continuous and many cuts – the subtitle "Director's Cut" should not be ignored. It should not be read as one more example of Modernism in poetry, but as the image of the paradox of complete freedom: non-alienation can be expressed only by transgression and deconstruction and their opposite, the obsession with claustration and destruction – M is likely to have been murdered.

Jean Bessière

THE GAR DEN

DIRECTOR'S CUT

LOUIS ARMAND

eyes lips dreams then night goes first nothing then night in the beginning before time in the confrontation of light & intractable unlight in the dawn of the word tangled in branches of TV static *wake up they've been expecting you* lying there in that solarised caress the very inverse of a woman prepared to mock her makers all aerials & elbows & hipbones & objectified spare ribs grubbying the seigniorial fingers licked till they gleam white as nativity talismans painstakingly erected out of so many test-patterned false starts white as an egg as a lamb's eye as boiled testes she can almost taste them enough to turn a goat's stomach what kind of thing was the beginning do the floodlights come magically on & *voilà* you're lying with your legs spread in the middle of a photograph of Utopia & sheets sweatsoaked wound in a truss from which a limp arm fernlike uncoils completing a shape that describes backwards one extremity to the other a dislocated ampersand or a bruised M tipped on its side or a semilegible Phrygian Phoenician Greek Σ or a K for *kafir* monogrammed on a piece of bloody sackcloth a ratty pillow a threadbare comforter that's come unstuffed cradled like a child's lifesize placebo on that fleabed in that closet-room moulded to within a standard deviation while tormented hands probe for the unresponsive vein the rote melancholy at its heart the poetic source from which a curdled sentimentality flows reaching for the vertigo of accomplished grace like some over-frigged *ficus* because one of the characteristics of things that're plainly visible in this world is they're not really seen at all but a woman isn't dumb matter animated one gram at a time from precognitive white noise a broken record under the hypnotist's needle a hologram with a mind-ray glitch in the Garden of Unearthly Delights miscreant among miscreated abjects waiting only to be taken in hand for the *shem* to be placed upon her forehead mouth tongue so as to sense to recall impressions *this* body *this* bed *this* room though being itself nothing but phonetic gibberish muttered foreignly from afar turned to dopplereffect *yeux lèvres rêves* a preceding echo a voice beside itself plagiarised by its significations the way Allah's braille-fingers mysteriously upon

His keyboard & words words words puking *spilling out of nowhere* in cataracts of limelight & all things holy writ that any second now every takfiri within a hundred mile radius will be clamouring at her back door to serve notice of her culpability before the fact & corporeality after but it's never enough to be their *tabula rasa* as soon as you open your eyes they expect a miracle look it's child's play wanting a pitch-perfect nursery rhyme to come from your mutoid mouth the first dumb spoken syllables *mama caca dada* as if it's the metaphysical upheaval of poetry to insist on the verbal qualities of things the physical sense while prose belongs to the essential relations of the universe but what's it saying that pedantic oracle in your head *première nuit & donc jour* beginning with the first before all other nights & not just the one you can't remember *d'abord la nuit* beginning or ending it's all the same day night & then afterwards my pretty little pupil *faire face à cette autre cette réalité de la lumière qui résiste* because eyes these eyes your eyes needn't be open for any of this to be literally or metaphorically real & it's within her power she tells herself to refuse to say *je refuse* shaking off the barbiturate sleep-haze the hangover the tristesse postcoitum *ce corps ce lit cette chambre* & that voice *étrangère* insisting who or what & you feel *her* body lying tense

& silent hopeless & beside her an *other* body a cloying
doppelgänger created no doubt out of a prejudice for symmetry
& because first attempts are as a rule a failure *mon amour M*
listening to the unfamiliar rhythm of its breathing there in the
near-distance like wind coursing through the street broken
into an echo of an echo M for mute for *ma mère* for *morte* for
migraine morphine misery for money machine mantra
myxoma malaria for mongrel melanoma macabre morbid
mandragora for mastectomy for meanness martyr mastoid for
moaning bitchbody for missed messiah for manhole for
Mam'selle X mindwash & milk of human miserliness for
momentary marred mutilated for all the malediction &
menace & melodrama punctuated by most complicit silence
& the silence around that silence like an echo in suspense in
pure *mise en scène* that calls back aloud *en silence* to significations
blotted-out snuffed during that endless preceding night into
which everything she isn't permitted to remember gets sucked
its black parentheses never more than *the blink of an eye away*
the non-time of its enclosing cadence but what's it saying that
black mouth radiant at the end of her mind its too-heavy
consonants *ses accords noirs* sinking discordant one into another
like waves around a wreck an unmeaning but relentless rhythm

seizing pulling translating the instant again & again & again & again *mort finitude détermination négativité* in restless & frustrated monotone *une monotonie turbulente* whatever you want to call it obscuring her thoughts or what she thinks are her thoughts *confusing them* she opens her mouth & tries to speak becoming a past tense I'm getting ahead of myself she says but only in her head only in a manner of speaking *elle ouvrait la bouche & essayait de parler* shit do I have to listen to this all day every day *hello world come in are you receiving over* but nothing no-thing a dull empty sound a knot in the throat in the lungs *un son vide* knowing in reality that none of this belongs nothing belongs her thoughts her pleasure her body as ethereal as the magic cinema against the ceiling the wind in the curtains the pale light that flickers off on off on off on off on off on off on off on off in spastic shadowplay across the side of her face casting the mouth in darkness a dark cavity beneath the black rings of her eyes lips in the stammering light & outside a muffled cadence of footsteps passing beneath the window the obstinately ticking clock murmur of language entangled *strangely* because *inexplicable* like hair someone's not hers knotted around her tongue her face passively unresembling itself as all-of-a-sudden in a reflex she *opens her eyes* finally telling herself but only after the fact that she has no choice *open* she says & *voilà* a half-formed room in revolving tequila-yellow sunrise streaked red by eyelid-flutter 24 frames for each second minute hour how many frames would it take to depict a lifetime dedicated to pointless secrecy its most secret part the shadow under the lamp the space between the words the same space between different words or different spaces between the same words making hieroglyphs of unsaying engraved white upon white yielding if only as a formality to subtle spectrographies of self-divided light she pictures a kaleidoscope whose coloured shapes dissolve instantly on contact with air like a language you only dream in while your alter-egos are forced to go on living it 24/7 *on pain of death* no less that stepmother-tongue to her mechanical Cinderella sweeping out the ashpits of malevolent nonlife does she go there to escape or to surrender & be put out of her misery by someone anyone a complete stranger her Prince Charmless capable of a more definitive a more total violence she'd walk the length & breadth of the city on broken glass if only for the sweet blissful promise of conjugal braindamage already the bells are gonging in her ears but what'd be the *absolute minimum* for everything to be & remain incomprehensible forever like a poem written in words she can't hope to understand beginning with a line & then the line faltering panic arc of a seabird stranded too far inland the futile beating of imaginary wings there where the eye breaks off suddenly & falls from the page towards the bedsheet the floor the stairs the street the river the smell of leaves & wet earth mingling in the sharp smell of the tanneries & she feels herself once more listening far off to an echo of an echo listening for the first disconnected murmurings of day just before dawn actually breaks straining to recall what it looks like when the sun rises on the red lines of rooftops or their redness sinks beneath the sun to imagine what type of sound it makes dragging itself over the dark cut of the High Atlas the ringing of granite the sudden intonations of prayer *adhan* which is the call to listen *'dhina* penetrating the ear that listens *'udhun* immaculate as the most immaculate of conceptions to bear witness that there is no god *'an lā 'ilāha* but only the One prick finger cunt mouth anus sometimes in her dreams they used a hacksaw instead of poetry to cut her infidel body in half cut her hands off at the wrists the fingers joint-by-joint first fear then pain shock haemorrhage & this's the love thou bearest in the android cries of tortured amplified dawn morning midday afternoon night tied naked as Eve to the five pillars feet hands neck in the dust of the marketplace the fly-thickened hides of slaughtered camels perfuming the air as a crowd leers through the awnings the faces of tongue-lolling rutting dogs what does their Allah want shoving His *langueparole* into her without preamble as if thus to justly imitate life but what'd He know about it serenading Himself at His writingdesk for hours-on-end in beautiful phrasings no-one can understand having reduced everything to its elemental atomic kernel the pure words the secret language no-one to this day has succeeded in uttering not even their compassionate Allah their unthinkable Allah who no mouth anus cunt has ever sullied *al-Rahman al-Rahmin* but a woman too mustn't be heard mustn't be seen what would it prove if the blind without touching without listening could be made to believe in such a difference man & woman night & day *day* she murmured *night* as if either could mean anything after all something concrete a body *her* body *this* body a narrow band of perspiration about her wrist the air upon it cold as tempered steel brined leather piano wire when one of these hands touches the other is it true the things in question are my own bound to me as much as I'm bound to them because the guilty are punished or because the crime always befits the punishment these hands they'll say touch the same things because they're the hands of the one same body the things themselves the sullied presence speaking understanding hearing the sound of a typewriter entering from the adjoining room a dissonance of keys struck at irregular intervals yet all together in fluid symphony a palimpsest notes vibrating in air a naked body upon a bed in disarray a sheet of paper deeply indented & in places cut through bleeding exposing the barely legible traces of a subtext whose lines have either been crossed out with a similar violence or else appear to be dreaming themselves arranged as if in allegorical ecstasy crying *no* between clenched teeth lips *no* & choking on it because *no* means *nothing* means *please* means *yes* I will *yes* means *la règle faite pour être violée* if only to make it stop not even wishing everything in reverse but only to stop right there in the space between the images in the flicker of eyewhite & all her voodoo-mothers wading in blood re-endowed with lost powers of speech chanting fuck shit piss who'll buy a word for 100 *mitqāls* & in unison they howl *el feurdj* the slit *el keuss* the vulva *el kelmoune* the voluptuous *el ass* the primitive *ez zerzour* the starling *ech cheukk* the chink *abou tertour* the crested one *abou khochime* the one with the little nose *el guenfond* the hedgehog *es sakouti*

the silent one *ed deukkak* the crusher & *tseguil* the importunate
el fechefache the watering-can *el becha* the horror *el taleb* the
one-who-yearns *el hacene* the beautiful *en neuffakh* the one
that swells *abou djebaha* the projection *elouasa* the vast one *el
dride* the large one *abou beldoum* the glutton *el mokaour* the
bottomless *abou cheufrine* the two lipped *abou aungra* the
humpbacked *el rorbal* the sieve *el hezzaz* the restless *el lezzaz*
the unionist *el moudd* the accommodating *el moudine* the
assistant *el mokeubbeub* the vaulted one *el meusboul* the long
one *el molki* the duellist *el mokabeul* the ever-ready-for-the-
fray *el harrab* the fugitive *el sabeur* the resigned *el maoui* the
juicy *el moseuffah* the barred one *el mezour* the deep one *el
addad* the biter *el menssass* the sucker *el zeunbur* the wasp *el
harr* the hot one *el ladid* the delicious the cushion the pillow
the table the brushstroke Ô what engines of sorcery are these
invading her subconscious like abject DNA the thousand&one
horrors its takes to manufacture a birthcanal for whatever
selfproclaimed Son-of-Man happens to come along & wouldn't
that Christ's Y chromosome have been something to behold
mon dieu furtively masturbating itself the apple of His
mammy's eye I want to share this emptiness with you He says
facelessly staring down from the dead screen where the film's

meant to reflect the Promised Land the Perfumed Garden this Wilderness of Failure preferring nothing but a journey without direction & no conclusion & that disillusioned voice punctuating your thoughts when the light faded it says I went in search of myself there were many paths & many destinations one instant opening to another suddenly & with no apparent connection the stigmata confusing them or else she'd already gone on ahead turning pages like somebody who's forgotten about the words & has begun to move unconsciously among their meanings a lucidity hidden in the void a spectre you want to call out to there where she's already begun to vanish passing through a locked door but like the doors in dreams it has no handle as if to say there was an indecency which took shape in her & which held her at bay *le sacrifice le fidèle* turning as upon an instrument of torment & thus she dies while watching herself die one increment at a time one death one *petite morte* at a time towards the insurmountable paradox she's been secretly making love to all her life in consummated incest every one of her countless doppelgängers past & to come like literally dispassionate Persinettes Petrosinellas Rapunzels casting their divided mind out the window at the fairytale landscape while Allah sits there at His machine writing *them* in place of *her* in the persona of whatever available *Jeune Vierge autosodomisée par les cornes de sa propre chasteté* & wouldn't she've preferred a quiet picnic down by the rosebushes by the burbling brook in a springtime bower Ô of course she said yes unconsciously adhering to a belief in the principle of interchangeability but that wasn't really her those fragments notes treacherous insights on the way to some occasion some grotesque speculum of selfknowledge the consoling illusions of an Ultimate Rationale an Idea standing for a nullified Thing *un vide simultané* all that a cynical readership has sought to make her represent at one or another time in History this hovering back & forth between the imagined presence of an absent thing & the material presence of an imaginary absence *une absence de mots* & *une absence de choses* a monster with two faces in other words whose meaning pretends to elude you who've always understood the principle of *rien soutenu par rien* or better yet the nothing begotten of nothing of no-thing my sullen Cordelia like a face drawn in sand at the edge of the sea let us hasten to the appointed time that permits us to rejoin ourselves do you understand my life & my death don't belong to me *ce monstre à deux faces* who never ceases to charm with its vile delusions of happiness Ô for so long I've wanted to run

away to go off into the mountains in the most profound
depths of my darkness to piss in the darkness to howl in the
darkness among the women of my blood to be naked at the
rendezvous in the forest in a rented room on the Avenue
Mohammed V in a cage in the Djemalfnaa surrounded by
toothless crones obscenely caressing the mouths of glass jars
lubricated with spit a persistent circular motion of fingers
agitating the air into a squalling moan first it vibrates within
the ear then penetrates the entire body rising to a pitch of
unbearable arousal a punishment centred entirely in the ritual
of anticipation the storm that never breaks the strictures of a
connotation that's only ever intrinsic & such was she created
to suffer in endless public displays of humiliation like a bitch
squatting in its oestrus merely thinking it leaves her breathless
is this what you open your eyes for just to be able to stare into
the blackhole of *non je n'ai pas envie de ma mère* I'm born more
than once & die more than once whenever a poet imagines a
faint rustling in the intestines & pictures autumn leaves in a
landscape that's never seen spring well forty-thousand years is
a long enough time to call half of human memory but still *it*
knows nothing of the sea that particular sea which lay in virile
freedom where now *I* lie in the painted cave of a body others

have made in spirit only *buffalo-head antelope acacia solar-disc* my feet in Tazzarine my heart in Djebel Amour but Ô my love it's only disorder that wakes us the storm in the desert the sky aflame with the aurora of the Sahrawiya & now it rains salt gold slaves now the seed of Beni Hassān now fax machines landmines passenger jets broken ceasefires *civilisation is when you know your rights & are conscious of your duties* & if I've followed one by one all the steps of the route chosen neurotically going back to the start every time a doubt or suspicion directed me there in other words I haven't been allowed I haven't allowed myself to arrive at a single conclusion without having retraced all the thoughts that preceded it but is that even possible chance when I seek it's beyond my reach I could've said it escapes me but it's not from me that it escapes since I've never had it in my grasp & at the same time something resembling a memory-breakdown sets in I begin to be afraid of forgetting as though unless I made a note of everything I'd be unable to hold onto any part of it all these extraneous elements which are nothing more perhaps than elaborate arrangements of planes & facets & simultaneous aspects if only to project a sense of volume in space something tangible enough to frame a presence independent of impressions something beyond the dark codecs of Allah's pixel-eye seeing inward & outward simultaneously & from every conceivable angle but such deep complicity can't be expressed in words or else it's *all* that can be expressed in words & our intentions are merely a way of saying that these things don't belong to *us* lost inside the image-duplicator all her past selves lined up along the windowsill to watch her undress stroke herself penetrate herself to a dreary anticlimax how long had she been unconscious it's necessary they said to know the history of your history & not merely the too clear pain of sentimental love but such a thing remained cruelly distant cut-off frozen remote like rival circumstances fleeing from a mirror I turn & look & see myself lying there paralysed in robotic sleep limbs swaying above the prone image I realise with the unnerving clarity of intuition that this is the dreaded Somatic Cauteriser programmed to negate every one of my thoughts even this one & suddenly something was coming out of my throat a refracted shockwave a quote-unquote inhuman sound according to Allah's account but those who write always imagine they know the process first you disinfect the immediate area then calmly make an incision she could see His hands like the hands of a surgeon a pianist practicing scales up & down her exposed thorax Ô she'd make a flute out of his bones when He died & then see how He liked it the quickening pulse in the groin the white light in the brain thinking it was just a matter of floating up to the Pearly Gates & ringing the doorbell but in the meantime she'd just have to revenge herself on the bits she could clearly remember driving through El Moukef in the back seat of a taxi streets of bleached red dust wiping the sweat from her forehead she hadn't slept for too many days outside everything blurred erupting like celluloid a child with pustules covering its face thrust a bag of rotten oranges at the window *salt tears wound the child's blinded eyes* this day at last to be delivered *inshallah* but she was afraid of homelessness every time she dreamed of fucking Him being alone in the city without walls without windows naked in the street the glare staring back through a fume of haemorrhaged faces mouths mouthing *pity never helped the dead* over & over & telling herself it's not me they're talking about it's not the Lamb of Allah who was slain *faites revenir la viande d'agneau dans le beurre & l'huile assaisonnez avec les épices couvrez d'eau & laissez mijoter à feu doux la viande doit rissoler dans son jus en fin de cuisson* white as always symbolising purity of intent all those earnest directives to love & cherish the proverbial *we* who somehow are never required to bear the proverbial brunt there're always others to suffer in place of us to affirm their touching allegiance to so called reality like a golem's placenta buried beneath a pomegranate tree the future's always been alien but they expect us to get all teary-eyed about the past talking & forever talking about their clear analysis of the situation as naked as a billboard on the Boulevard el Mansour you'd've thought to hear it that a single prophylactic was tantamount to the whole nation's reproductive industry going out on strike & wasn't everybody's adolescence populated by nightmares of witchdoctors with wire coathangers chasing them through the medina of course they felt the whole world owed them something a martyr's paradise one two three steps into the emptiness but when I'm dead & turned to bugshit who'll play the scapegoat *mes camarades mes soeurs* expecting it for free & not gold frankincense myrrh lying there with your knees pressed against your forehead waiting for it to be over & done with the Doorway of Life she'd said unsmiling at Him how could she joke at a time like this as if just to exist she had to constantly explain herself answering when called standing to attention embodying an inventory of only generalised items despite a pretence to singularity M being for molecular migraine monstrous malady morbid for example the way when Allah unable to decide on an appellation for this ill-starred puppet simply wrote M on the back of her neck as in Madiha Maessa Mahasine Majda Maliha Maounia Mariem Menna Méret Milouda Morjana Mouina Mounira or any of the other preconscious harem he'd manifested out of His munificence the signified mystery of the feminine marasmus no less a starved wavering geometry hunched over a bathtub with a bloodied Gillette turning itself into a slaughterhouse a travesty with all the consistency of ground kofta oozing between strange fingers to be moulded & marinated & threaded on an ornamental skewer & every time she smelt the smell of cooked meat wafting up from the street vendors it made her want to puke the fat pooling in the gutter the gorged mouths juice spilling from chins their keen tongues could taste her lying up there in her room in the fetid heat of herself serenaded by the flies *let the dead eat the dead* she cried but Allah couldn't hear her over the whirr of tyres the taxi changing down through its gears as it climbed as it descended leaning with her face half-buried in the brown upholstery an engorged blowfly on the window watching with its horrible eyes it wasn't enough to be eaten alive now they had to lay their eggs in her

the fly-eyed imams of Mouassine surveying the traffic with

their oiled beards combed & perfumed flaunting themselves

along the café terraces *réservé pour les hommes* on their chairs

spread-kneed under female djellabas their hookahs & tongues

up each other's arses *allons enfants* you have your slender little

penises to tend for your admiring mothers the maître d' with

a tattoo beneath one eye like anthracite you'd need a heart of

stone to accept the money of men every hour of the day staring

at a twisted thumbnail at the mole inside the crook of her

thumb her naked shoulderblade against the rough seatcover

daylight between red roofs the sky too hidden *why am I taking*

so much time it's the wheels' fault she can't keep her mind on

what she's thinking the drone & heave the building to a climax

& breaking off a woman's supposed to go mad punctually not

by anachronism but what could she say for herself with Him

sitting there beside her in front of her behind her with His

girlish fingers pressing the buttons of His cosmic controlboard

massaging the keys twitching the wires playing her like a

marionette M did this M thought that M bore her puny soul

for anyone to read for anyone to perv at like a spread centrefold

with its gloss thumbed off a paralysed hopeless thing with a

hole where the lepidopterist's pin jostles her intestines Ô my dear being fucked by Allah must be a fulltime occupation *doth she protest at being thus honoured above all women to be the receptacle of His rapture* moaning into her pillow that her bleeding heart isn't just some petrified piece of History for tourists to come & gawk at the jutting minarets & the mountains surrounding it the garish souks the snake-charmers acrobats potion-peddlers the swirling of kebab smoke between her thighs holds the promise of incomparable sensations & exotic North African charm but these emotions are descriptive not logical at times she imagines herself changing place with Him becoming Allah a contractual arrangement she whips Him five times a day He cooks & cleans her soiled underwear she wonders how Eve didn't croak of boredom day-one & decides it was revenge booking her ticket out of Papa's playroom when He came in that day & found Little Brother with a mouthful of custard apple *takdim watikat al-istiqlal* they shouted & now they too were free to walk among the dead as other men are in fraternal suffrage their ingenuous circles of hell their harems their serenading pricks & in her eyes the mullahs were dancing waving their painted cardboard signs BELIEF IS THE OPIATE OF THE UNEQUAL *inshallah* we are all solemn promises they sing but in the

crowded room she can barely hear them she's trying to push
her way to the door to get to the Gare de M_________ on time
for the last train for the only way back but when finally she
reached the station platform a woman stepped in front of her
& instead of moving to the side she allowed her body to come
into contact upsetting her balance & when she touches her she
resents her because her touch is cold it reminds her of her
betrayals because even compassion etc the cruelty of it the
falseness of it like glass this woman who's really *her* like all the
other women she's desired but in front of an audience she
finds it impossible to suspend her own disbelief *I know that
you're words I know that you're reading me* the station windows
in which the platform folds back in reverse like a folio with
stage-directions crammed into the margins between every line
undoing the dialogue to the point of becoming it *strophe
antistrophe* one foot up one foot momentarily down in
empathy alternating with aversion alike in the eyes of a keen
observer to a sadistic metronome her arm slicing the air left-
to-right as she falls to the ground in a panicked & exaggerated
movement producing an effect of isolated melodrama in the
midst of an opera the swirling chorus & stagehands & the
rebellious orchestra climbing over the audience to reach the

exit in a lockstep of spasmodic passion & lo the sea of swaying bovine faces parted & she saw her debilitation lying there in ceremony like a simple script-note wreathed in miniscule shorthand explaining that it's in the nature of an object to excite feelings of horror anger fear despair expressed by an audible grinding of teeth a raised eyebrow a wrinkled forehead lips pressed firmly especially in the middle a kind of smile of clenched indignation between jaws of disdain thus is a single action midwife to multitudes telling them *it wasn't me* but still they clamoured for life for breath for His fatherly attention for their thirst to be slaked for the hand that feeds The Gracious The Merciful yes but an unstable mind's an evil thing in a moment she'll be begging Him Ô daddy I've changed please don't be frowny daddy take me with you & He a prisoner trapped between the walls of her accusatory look mumbling incoherently now that the audience has joined in demanding its pound of flesh a raised hand in the spotlight & something glinting in it the programme indicates here that the head of the animal is first aligned with the Qiblah & slaughtered fast upon utterance of the Bismillah its blood drained like an unresolved sentence no sooner written than groping automatically for the backspace to exe the whole thing out the simplest thing of course would be to just make her disappear

if such a thing could be gotten away with & not have to delete

her one line at a time M then N V I then nothing a blank

paperspace but such things are almost always gotten away with

like a rote accumulation of erased lost vitiated Time pushing

against the edges of the page *catastrophe antistrophe* filling the

emptiness of that absurd *mise en scène* like an understudy in

the wings diligently rehearsing other sentiments than her own

always saying what she's made to say tormented by the

stupidities of others their words entering her body taking

possession of it so that she can neither see nor think falling to

the floor & crawling fishbellied on the muddy linoleum face

smeared with dirt Ô you who believe do not go near prayer

when you are intoxicated till you know well what you say or if

you have touched woman & can't find water to bathe betake

yourself of pure earth & wipe your face your hands surely

Allah is forgiving but at the last minute He stretches out His

hands to stop her from falling a reflex or an afterthought but

never soon enough the faces crowding ever-closer on the

platform & trains rushing past out of conjured darkness

shuddering stripping back the air & the downwards motion of

her body caught frame-by-frame torquing against the light

how cinematic death was when it wasn't real with its *culpa meas* stuck in its throat but you'd be an idiot to talk like that when in real-life people just stand there laughing or shitting themselves or cringing like some diva with a urinary tract infection stopping the camera at the exact moment her head struck the concrete with her eyes staring straight back at Him jarred suddenly out of focus as if it would've made any appreciable difference reaching that turning point one day or any other day with a note written out & folded in her pocket taking one last look in the mirror before slipping outside & finding a taxi to take her to the train station checking the timetable before walking across the crowded platform to stand at the furthest point & wait for the next train so she could step in front of it but what if she didn't & instead of sneaking out of the hotel room took the key out of the lock & calmly stripped off her clothes & lay down again beside that *other* & closed her eyes again would she allow herself to be overcome by so little pain *I'm cold* she stammered *I'm shaking* lifting her hand to her face with the gesture of a marionette *I can't stop shaking* she pressed her languishing eyes with her knuckles & rocked the weight of her body back & forth on the edge of the bed & there were moments hours sometimes days when she'd stand by the window compulsively snatching the curtain back & staring into the street to catch her secret adversaries *in flagrante delicto* & they indefatigably obliging her with their presence a constant flow a moveable feast of kufis taqiyahs tarbooshes of burnouses djellabas gandoras of calloused feet sandals babouches dragging through fetid cesspools rivers of grey mud as putrid as their masterful sperm their embarrassed fishpaste five-times-a-day polishing their foreheads with it their fat raisins their sultanas at the same time she lulls them into a state of unsuspecting desire & while they're secretly fucking her in their minds she imagines them dead like wingless birds teetering over involuntary terrains bleakly absurd looking down onto the street nothing more than a glance an instant of recognition to cancel the oppressive weight of the night sometimes I don't know if I want to live or die sometimes it's painful not to die haha if only at last to be done with words to be able to resolve everything into a single continuous *non* like a rope thrown to a drowning man like flowerless stems hanging in a glass bowl on the windowsill *car il y a tant de choses que je n'ose pas te dire tant de chose que tu ne me laisserais pas dire* now their shadows rise & fall & lie flat where the sun touches on the leaf-coloured water now a figure

stirs in the bed & the room separates into light & solid planes
& things unhinge from nowhere & in an infinitesimal fraction
of a moment a passionate demand for justice surges upwards
from the bowels of the people & Allah is moved to satisfy it
like the Lion of the Rif when *his* blood was up sprinkling her
cunt with coriander & white sugar a hunchback vaulted like
an arch serenading Babylon with His sonorous kisses Ô the
exquisite sweet flow of saliva in that otherwise soundless
odourless colourless utopia as dreamlike as the Tangier Stock
Exchange knowing that paying one's way is related to the wish
to defecate upon one's masters rising up in the world on
Archimedes' screw *property's an illusion* He says as once more
morning replaces dawn night into dawn into morning
suspended in that single moment all moments interceding &
over the city the sky becomes a fire a burst ventricle loudhailers
& trucks & voices pealing in chorus she felt the light beat
against her eyelids little by little a red disk filling the black
screen & faint blue vertical & horizontal lines weaving spectral
acrostics of Xs & Ys between the membrane & the eye neither
time now nor space in a controlled loss of control but if Allah
starves He can always eat His children while for everyone else
meaning's simply eclipsed did they think an AK47 & a

dictionary would deliver Paradise or merely retribution for

someone else's sins a mirror's just a piece of glass whichever

way you look at it nothing but angles of incidence & angles of

reification & not the exterminating angels she'd once believed

hid themselves behind the silvery sheen like Death behind its

mask waiting to catch her by surprise *in flagrante delicto*

observing her lips to tremble & redden & her eyes to become

languishing as self becomes antiself becomes an echo only a

conjurer's cheap trick as if to say *open sesame* & there she was a

wax fetish with needles sticking out a sliver of mock moon

through a barred window the Madonna of Al-Mansur in an

open hospital tunic *dear Allah I'm so desperate no money no-one

wants to fuck me please send help M* as though she'd seen a ghost

the way she might've expected someone her saviour like Jean

Genet to appear suddenly on the gravel driveway wearing

flowers in his hair she might've run outside one day past the

guards as if to greet him a moth flying blindly into light & that

was Death & all that filthy hygiene they'd injected her with

day & night spilling out like spilt milk like crème-de-menthe

how picturesque if she were still alive she'd have to stomp on

them the tiny day-glo fishheads stomp them to death death

death bare feet white against the white of the massacred

concrete while Petit Déjeuner recites the verses he's just composed *ah ah you're hideous lean forward & look at yourself in my shoes* the lights flicker & the entire sky flickers as well the driveway is needlessly cluttered & false it sets M's teeth on edge in opposition to the languid grace her mouth affects as it slides forward then retracts sucking in His presence she starts to unfasten her arms & legs till she's nothing but a spectator *is this what true pain is* she tries to hate herself but can't escape the feeling she's only following commands in order to hate & to love there must be two at least how lonely Allah must've been before He created her to suffer for Him but how could she be sure who was who anymore doubt having a tendency to always flower in the mind on opportune occasions Allah she decides mistreats her because He despises her now that He's had possession of her body what more does Man want with a woman but to negate the rest as well like pissing into a bidet & when Genet raises his bare arm she feels the muscle twitch in her own arm *the only true thing is play-acting* she said in a low submissive voice whereupon Genet showed he was satisfied *go on be sarcastic* but that wasn't reason enough to kill her He'd abandon her too like all the rest hadn't Allah seen her in fact lying there in a heap trying to touch His hand to speak to Him *promise me* she'd said but He hadn't been moved to promise He could promise nothing He promised nothing as remote it must've seemed as the Pillars of Hercules *her sickness did this to her not I* a woman of course is always sick whenever she's not the obliging memory of *les temps perdus* sick of life sick of the night of day sick of being the alibi of Allah's unexamined *sale-con-science* His intimate soul His *cinéma théâtre roman opéra* lying there she reminds Him of a broken TV the way her face flickered in the light like the simile of an image with part of the colour spectrum drained out but can an image alone be capable of denying nothingness of taking precedence over life *la rencontre la passion physique la séparation le retrouvaille* He's trying to convince Himself of a belief that when He looks at her she's really there but memory has no obligations her eyes are telling Him the world was ever the way it was they say the world in which a path had been prepared for Him leading as if inexorably to this travesty dreamt-up in an operating theatre *Messieurs Mesdames* they've cut her out & replaced everything inside with a faulty machine *tragedy* He wrote *has become indistinguishable from farce* sweating into His collar afraid He too might be contaminated by it the very air felt thick with her disease like some sulphurous cave the words took form credulously before His eyes *a philosophical study into the condition of the soul* how fear doth make the intellect valiant & that idiot Sartre with an octopus for a brain telling that Man must suffer on *his* own behalf while hydrogen bombs & fast-breeder reactors & Simone de Beauvoir naked in Chicago in M________ they discuss the fate of the world also confusing existence with life when did it begin where was the first green place they found slouching out of the deserts of Africa Arabia Palestine dragging their feet across Euphrates clay & set down in an orchard the likes of which unseen to forget the horrors of the path by which they'd come the murderous ape the receding ocean to wash their consciences clean from now on they said the world's right in front of us we no longer need to create it & the ibis-women nodded & sang knowingly in their incomprehensible voices in their forbidden dialect History reserves a special place for them slanted in the retelling *Le Meurtre de Gonzague* enter Sultan & Sultanah very lovingly upon a bank of *fleur de raisin* the proles applaud they're hungry there's nothing they'd rather eat than the tripe of aristocrats but Power has a way of displaying its charms a Sultan's employed to die pompously for the good of all a woman to weep *purpose* she cries *is but a slave to memory* so long ago according to the copyright she appeared even to herself as an allegory all these years later forgetting which was the actual crime & which was the punishment husbanding the strange fruit or lying down with Allah's first-born His belovèd son-&-heir His gormless infatuated golem impatient for his first fuck her lips tasting of mint tea & pomegranate & disillusionment *je ne trouve pas je cherche* & He of course suspecting none of this her tendency to become psychotically depressed carving serpentine patterns on her skin with flaked obsidian intentions don't change she told Him they only become more apparent descending by predictable steps to slammed doors screams & smashed glass in the night eventually rape becomes a methodology a conjugal routine such as washing dirty socks barehanded it's possible to be sentimental about anything if you put your mind to it like endless handcuffs & leather harnesses & rubber truncheons the cuffs had left permanent gauge marks on her wrists & ankles the torn skin across her thighs step-by-step the scenario created its own outcomes stumbling in the wilderness of an Eternal Punishment she'd been secretly longing for from the moment she exited the womb in that unconscious groping for words to appease to acquiesce to suffer is this all there is now nothing but appeasement language disinformation sometimes she dreams of a knife that all her doppelgängers had one neck so she could put them out of their misery & afterwards she could still taste the electricity in her mouth the metal in the blood her tongue like a botched castration she leered she made obscene grimaces in the glass she spread consternation 100mg at a time shitting in the ward corridor a thin sliver of watery grey & thus beholding her bestial state Allah was beside Himself not because of the dishonour brought upon Him but from the tedium of the stereotype & in response they tie her hands & feet forcing her into an ungainly abasement He can see the shaved patches of scalp the groove in her cheek from the leather thong dead voltages stir behind her eyes as they gaze upon His hideous face without recognition no-one remembers the old story how in the beginning there was no-thing only a word not even a word how could the universe in its infinity have spoken a shout in the street a shot fired randomly into a crowd the soundless Big Bang light fleeing through the same void it creates more alone than ever *it's the future that decides if the past's alive or not* every spent-breath struggling to exhume it from banality & wouldn't this be perfect happiness if I opened my eyes to see *as if for the first time* a vision that's existed forever the original electron perhaps but when she

opened her eyes in reality the room the street the city had been

replaced by their opposites as if they'd all been reconstructed

backwards in a studio in the memory of a video-cam or

microsatellite shaped like an angel beaming its pixelated POV

on Paradise Lost inverted in time or reversed in space *to cloak*

the memory of all the terrible explosions & crimes perpetrated by

Men with the faces of children & the tears & smiles of women

while the Director chides them for their lack of realism the

question is to act or to be while to choose is impossible trapped

inside her Kaspar Hauser impenetrability ogling the world

through a slit in a mask as if it were the last hiding place on

earth a shelled mollusc a crab in a vagina all for the love of

nothingness zigzagging up into her intestines from that

delicately pleated anus dilating & contracting under a magical

remote stimulus & the electrodes inside her head singing in

falsetto where the brainstem had become detached now

floating above her somewhere among the clouds of singed

flesh ozone burnt diesel excrement kif like the all-pervasive

au-de-cologne of *Allah-le-Tout-Puissant* pouring His morose

soul into His writing-machine whole consternated reams of

celibate marshland or thalidomide children or birds & sick

dogs or at night nothing but smoke or black & red insects or eyes fixed on the ground or spitting into the fire or the reeds & rushes or at the edge of the water in the coolness or the sway of androgynous hips or eyelashes or mouths filled with fever & desire or marked by secret depravity or rain falling like night on the sea or in the freezing dawn or the moon or in a rubbish pile but she was hormonally sick of poetry why couldn't words simply be described by things the nurse's saffron-stained hands for example the naked street urchin staring from the doorway for example the transvestite cop swinging his stick for example the prognathous imam with soap residue in his beard for example the Coca-Cola sign reflected in a spreading pool of donkey's piss for example the dog flicking its ears for example the refrigerated vial pierced by a hypodermic for example the callus at the base of her spine for example the hum of the rheostats for example the square root of -1 for example & with a simple flicking of a switch the entire ceiling came down forcing the breath out of her pinioned beneath an earthquake a hot wind coursing through the obliterated hallways & corridors through the impossible crevices of piled rubble pouring into her tonguing her eyes mouth the purple blinking neon of her gashed body is this what pleasure is defecating all

over her how far removed she's become from that image she
once had of a real woman & not this invisible travesty choking
in a cellar if only she could free herself she'd take a knife to her
throat drown herself with progestones estrogens antiandrogenes
in the name of their prophet amen *& mes fesses tu les aimes mes
fesses* I felt I was being pushed further & further down my
head my whole body till the pain had no feeling at all as if I
was a vagina giving birth to myself submerged & distant voices
echoing in unison further & further down like ghosts of
sunken Atlantic u-boats *no sleep all our memories are wasted
we're living dying inside a film to an audience of power stations* in
the future there'll be nothing but allegory extinction the vast
wrought signs of abolition sex not opposites coeval energies
wave-particles reproducing re-evolving we weren't the first
won't be the last newtlike in febrile amnesiac sea-voyage
through endless minefields a lit butane lamp in a room
thronged with giant moths how can anything endure the
terrible rising of the sun the semaphores of erupting heavens
of capitulated Time in the time of capitulation a dog-rose
blooming on the wadi where it doesn't belong are *love &
political meaning* incompatible the part played by fable in
transposing dramatic theory the wild nights they spent fucking

or roaming from place to place & bivouacking wherever they happened to be at dusk beneath the stars founding a nation on their bedrolls under the gunwales of their upturned ships or became barbarous nomads refusing even sleep sowing the desert littoral with their weeds & the wind's cultivating chaos here a bowl of broken glass light catching the shards a rusted pitchfork-head with tines threaded through hollow rocks driftwood crosses amulets hinges no fence to keep in or out the wind through wire harps keening singing moaning across the Rif the *malim* the talking pipes of Bou Jeloud what were they saying those shingle-voices those magic circles of white flint sandstone mudbrick redgreybrown the self-altering ash the alkaloids of apocryphal weather of tides & continental drift the sanctuaries of desiccated sea-kale the shadows of the eucalypti shaken by the ceaseless harmolodic stream flowing circulating throbbing feeding the spiral of scabious cistus horned-poppy valerian lavender & the bees the bees the bees she leans against the wall flattens her torso so they won't see her counting backwards from a hundred everything in its own time the Death-of-the-Gods wasn't because of *her* there were others suiciders faith-healers all pleading their innocence like the music she'd heard long ago in the Jardin de Bab El Kmiss

imagining all the things unseen & unspoken that haunted
each moment in immobile flux *guilty guilty* they cried *till
punished* they sang *guilty in the absolute* they who mitigate the
crime commit the crime *sub specie aeternitatis* as if knowing
their sequence of commands by heart without ever having
read or heard like cosmic background radiation the first future
tense but words are just mirrors of pervading entropy heat-
haze over distant rooftops dogs barking at debris of fallen
satellites what more can I hope for than to die unknown even
if pain's inescapable as ingrown as a thing within itself as
longing assault lament *who are you when you're inside me* even
in solitary confinement her eyes become lost in starlit skies
chest rising up towards her throat her gorge blackens the hole
of the navel the furrow of the larynx bruised with sweat as she
fluctuates among her alteregos I turn the page & there she is
again struggling with her mind that's been changed without
her permission invisible TV waves scrambling the live-feed *like
downloading the universe one telegraph signal at a time* if she
closed her eyes she could see the picture-lines descending her
retina like a tattoo being printed out inking itself scribing
itself into the *cahier du refuge* of her inner-being socalled like
dreamless kitsch & had she too become a fulcrum of their

controversy hesitantly poised upon the dereliction of the cosmos from quark to quasar & those ravaged shoulders of hers pinioned in reverse prayer *dear Allah why don't you see me anymore can't we just be casual acquaintances & fuck occasionally I miss your cock your fatherliness my eyes are so bad tonight is it because memory equals disappearance I still need to find out how to go further find clarity please please please write to me come back amen* but even supplication failed in its effect as she herself was failing & thought of all the people whose eyes would never meet hers across empty intersections & all the disregarded phrases from foreign languages blown through empty streets thronging her dreams with their fugitive existence how their voices both lured & repelled her *but did I create Allah before He created me* the way He'd taken such a shine to her queenly cunt glittering in the first light before coming to resemble in those long wilderness years a Bedouin's irrigation ditch but a Writer dies just like anyone else disappearing without a trace inside His words all future memories automatically deleted the only possible surface was to fill in the blanks to have something to hold onto somewhere to breathe this *histoire d'Ô je n'habitais pas la vie mais la mort* submitting with a docility close to that which binds a hypnotisee to her hypnotist it was too perfectly in accordance with the genre the way she accepted each sadistic humiliation & silence like a knot gathering each fragment of her consciousness into a point of dark interiority *they say I knew Him* but who really knows what they know His back to the camera in a blue headscarf in a photograph taken on the edge of the Sahara somewhere near Zagora maybe & the grey suit jacket that He wore everywhere till it fell apart like an allegory Art & Life the same narrow cut of the shoulders the way He hunched over His writing-machine wasting one illegible ream after another in pointless violence if all He'd wanted to do was make her into fiction He could've just turned once to look at her *l'incarnation de Sa part maudite* in all her intractable purity but for me I'm beyond words I've seen too much a woman's seductive enjoyment can just as easily be a mountain to subjugate in everlasting ascent *je rampe le long de ses contours* though it'd be easier just to clench her teeth forced back into an inner turmoil without revolution into the intermezzo of an existence that isn't nothing merely so a circle can be drawn around it singing like a child in the forest in such a very short time even her DNA will be illegible a nucleus of mutability in the same way as every word leads to something else a doorway a passage a sex a genesis doing everything it can to make itself beautiful *mon amour* & not just because Art's all

that remains of History like an endless supply of Fra Angelicos

ringed with a gold nimbus you'd think He'd choke on the

sentimentality if it weren't for the fact you ache to feel His

cum burning inside you my mythical female reader dutifully

conveying this nightly in your prayers on your raw knees as

nakedly as language permits the secret garden beneath the

ramparts beneath the burning gate & even though you have

no name for it this place exists like a temporary reprieve where

everything & its opposite narrow to a single arch doorway

windowpane in a room closed off from the senses the way its

walls expected nothing the illusions of the night before & the

night before that all absolved in lines of lips eyes bodies a

visceral thread created by a silence more intent than it should've

been to stitch time to reweave the departures & absences a

length of gutstring to tune an orchestra upon it was the same

night she always experienced over & over cut down the middle

like an anatomical display from which her very existence

diverged with all the ungainliness of a propaganda that

animates naked bodies in forensic mutual violence miming

the discrepancy between what's on show & that it's on show *les*

yeux ne veulent pas en tout temps se fermer their subterfuge has all the contradictory arousing qualities of death fear action dreams of the limits & banality of dreams watching them makes her laugh despite her vertiginous arousal thinking of all the women of mythology abducted by aliens in the throes of some erotic disorder one minute they're having their brains fucked out by a hirsute Lesbian the next they're in a plexiglass cocoon in Allah's private space laboratory hahaha she plays the more lurid details backwards & forwards through her mind savouring them out of a spite that's at best paradoxical knowing how He hears all sees all her personal Allah *no more love no more suicide* to repudiate is to lie yet taken objectively it assumes a false repose like the sacred dildo swelling against a thigh a hand against the small of the back Allah chides the lowliest molecule His hidden powers catch fire in a whirlwind of cracked milk-white tongues in the black blood of rapturous gall bladders He grows to enormous proportions inside her light & shadow in all their turmoil filling her senses allowing herself to surrender again despite knowing she's nothing but a substitute one among an infinite number for that Mother-of-God of His the famous recipient of untold pleasures but was *she* a woman or is there no such thing *per se* because the becoming of Allah in His licit & illicit Oedipal *jouissance* shouldn't be thought of as belonging to the woman category if only because it's never that simple to be a real infidel you need to be a paranoid schizophrenic as well as denying the quasi-hysterical identification of her orgasm with His *for god's sake look at this filth* did they really expect her to believe the war between the sexes wasn't sexual but transsexual the struggle for the phallus the threat of castration but the real mantrap was the separation between erotic themes & social themes the way at precisely such moments He put His hand between her legs & roughly began to caress the absence the hollow the hole the lack in which her being languished huddled like a shadow in a cave forever awaiting fulfilment by His supernatural light this Love that goes right through her unleashing panic agony dreams sometimes she has some of the most disgusting dreams in which nothing's left to chance as if every scenario had been thought-out in advance by an ego-maniacal computer with infinite RAM rotely intent on exhibiting its genius for industrialised punishment routines like some knot of overdetermination or an insideout blackhole whose fascination is that it constantly repels in order to conceal its monotonous singularity its *démultiplication catégorielle* made from the mannered vocabulary syntax meaning of a minor state functionary obliged by circumstances to prostitute himself in the souk as a letterwriter disconsolately arrayed at his typing machine *To Whom It May Concern* like some Grand Vizier brought face-to-face with the alienations of skilled labour it's a timeless gospel he wastes none getting down the first paragraphs of an epic in the making & no way shy about it a few days of punching the keys should provide ample substance for a compassionate pantomime he'll be able to milk till doomsday the poor Misunderstood Genius he surely is *does this remind you of anyone* she demands turning to the audience but words weren't made to last forever when you look in a mirror you don't see who's been there before you as if to keep something by denying it by denying the loss of it *like Hermione of her Longings & Lear of his Madness* & if the sudden apparitions come to life it's only in order to pass away it won't've been the last time art was born of coercion or innuendo sketched rather than achieved like lightning in a serene sky for a brief moment the world was on fire & her with it *Ô mirror mirror* but can you blame her with no word-machine of her own at her beck-&-call & having to make do with the primordial elements & less ancient artificial intelligences chased from their grottos & caves & oases to shelter under eaves in drains behind the walls inside the glass as like microwaves across cosmic solitudes their voices in many aeons unechoed *qui êtes vous* but she can only hear them as long as you believe in her like a sixth sense surrounded each of her actions yet not of their accord the witchcraft of retreating angles of bifurcated presences fleeting enough never to be remembered or misread or ignored the ever-selective works of unelected hours recurring in a suspended alien moment a culmination without conclusion as though each time she glimpsed only one aspect of the reality in which she's suspended but which she can't seem to grasp hold of adrift on an allegorical sea of her own devising with only the vaguest suggestion of landfall far in the distance carob trees of apparently real hair a sunken ship on a reef smoke signals deleting the sky above a once-extinct volcano dissolving to mirage she'd been counting the false sightings for days weeks the flocks of seabirds hinting at invisible shorelines luring her on hopelessly towards a shadowy stillness or a cloud-bank stubbornly retreating over the horizon like a movable mountain range each night the pale zodiacs flickering low in the east like campfires hidden deep in dark mangrove estuaries as she moved inexorably towards them swimming through the air insect-like in lunar trance but inevitability is its own illusion

even the Earth going around in circles the dark vital signs of
time-&-space the turmoil-without-purpose these little acts of
futility in which melodrama enlarges itself *this is the world I
am making use of in my reconfiguration* said the chrysalis to the
imago we live we die what's the Mind's part in all of this it
seems we exist the same way we dream in a world where the
old beauty is no longer beautiful but the new truth is not yet
true my love you are like a corpse from which the brain has
been removed & only foot-peddles levers hydraulic gears how
can anyone take themselves seriously with a toilet-chain up
their arses praying to the out-of-sync dimming light of the
Vision Splendid the Pejorative Vision the Contemplative
Non-Distance between a woman & the idea of a woman like
a vapour trail cutting enigmatically across the blue an ascent
towards something implicit & evasively banal that never ceases
to return like a dream-within-a-dream you reach out your
hand & the image of you reaching out your hand immediately
becomes a physical thing you're nevertheless utterly unable to
grasp because like any gesture it's a compilation of uncertainties
a hand a face *this* hand *this* face nothing is a foregone conclusion
crossing-out her lines so that she's forced to improvise in front
of the mirror as in the beginning hahaha the first-last refuge of

a woman-between-men the first stages of a terminal disease
but power also operates in its withdrawal from the scene the
vacuum of injustice between rich & poor between Africa &
Europe between man & woman she reaches her mouth across
the divide pressing her lips against the screen made warm
moist clouded by her breath to kiss the image of herself eat her
words is there a language that can express the *jouissance* of a
mouth crammed with vitriolic html where does the light go
that finds the retina dreaming of unique downloadable
character sets as though they stood on the verge of an
irrevocable erasure like a codename of which all that remains
is the initial letter a barely audible consonant alone in a sea of
noise indistinctly murmuring & beyond it the silence it masks
& which envelops it in the same precarious instant she felt
herself drawn towards it & repulsed lured by chance outlines
& pushed back & in that strangely present tense of her
oscillation she appeared to herself as a pair of eyes drifting in
their own space punctuating it but through which space also
flows & she was staring down at the streetlights aware that a
tide was welling up inside her & no longer a surface to reassure
only a reflection in the glass pierced by streetlights beyond the
punctured womanly form swelling to incredible proportions

of its own accord into a nebula of flesh & corrupted matter an idea began to take shape her body was a hive of wounds pre-existing any implement a secret mutilation from within *is this what it means to give birth* hahaha as though I'm always going back over something I can't recall because it's been *taken from me* & the fear that there's no end to this pantomime by retreating from the mirror one goes deeper into it by retracing one's steps one continually advances & at moments when her mind was quite clear she'd complain of the most profound darkness in her head of not being able to think of becoming blind & deaf of having two selves a real one & a false one which forced her to behave badly she felt she was struggling towards some haven of finality the secret unseen light in which the end would be revealed *lumen luminis* deciphered at last from the sidereal or hieratic writings of the lost chambers of night the places where the souls the divine entities the shadows & spirits the transfigured dwell symbols words phrases like talismans magic charms written over bodies of dead language the voices in the head the blankness & rage the conferred invisibility of the foresworn *inshallah* but how the revived syllable doth stink raised from its interred posture fumigated in dung like a gaping vulva they must bathe their language in red myrrh & myrtle-water in lavender & musk-rose-water in

boiled locusts & the bark of the pomegranate tree a whole

apothecary's bag of tricks how blessèd they must be who have

a god half the planet venerates down there between their legs

24hrs daily the sacred logos fresh as the proverbial daisy

pushed up from six feet under what a travesty Jesus-Lazarus

must've been with his wormy flyblown stigmata they never

paint Him that way planted atop Golgotha in the full sun all

the blood & unloosed bowels of the crucified wafting upon

the airwaves to any among the faithful of Judea with a nose to

smell by Ô hark an angel bearing floral-aldehyde number 5 a

melting winter note at 40° celsius *a woman's perfume with the

scent of woman* but to experience oneself as cut-off is also to

hold open the possibility of transcending this isolation by

entering into all those other lives savouring them like a mirror

in which no division of time or space prevails only the fluid

contour of its languid gaze tracing a path between each of her

gestures now opaque now transparent as half-formed celluloid

images in which the subject is forever moving beyond the edge

of the frame their features indistinct blurred unfocussed *as if I

were haunted by everything I am forbidden to remember* &

somewhere she was sitting on a bench by a river that resembled a photograph of the Seine & she was smoking a cigarette watching the barges slip by on the Lethe-waters below the stone parapets there are elements of a scene too much like a filmstrip left on the cutting room floor by going back over details perhaps it would be possible to reconstruct events & she was looking across at the people on the other side of the river there was something disturbing about their movements at a distance their mouths which seemed to open & close silently like fish a chorus of the damned who're drowning who can't even drown *nothing's real* she tried to scream but her voice had the quality of an overdubbed cassette as if she were on stage faking her own pain not laughing her legs flung open to the sun in one of her dreams Allah appeared to her as a walking melanoma done up in drag a blonde wig teeth plastic tits His neon bleeding lips reminding of vague deliriums formulated in the crudest medical terms a mask of voluptuousness weakness depression lethargic torpor *desire's ever-shifting* Allah said as too the mind which remains open to vision even when the eyes are not if something doesn't exist you have to make it exist sticking a coathanger up His arse His little abortions all tumbling out small & sticky & sad-looking dead like the world she wanted to kiss them make them better with tears in her eyes & a song in her loins & disco lights in constellation high over the Atlantic on a clear night if you looked hard enough you'd see the beacon atop the Empire State Building my child American dollars whisper in your dreams *This Land is Our Land* conducting their sacred product ceremony to bless the fecund with junk so they may bring forth degenerate multitudes like a callused mouth making love to a toothless conscience Africa was born at the intersection of two nightmares we think we're dying of grief but it's grief that dies of us exacting a kind of revenge in uneven stages the way a bone breaks & the tendons the muscles the arteries & the skin break also but not in a straight line nor afterwards grow back together at the same time lying there irradiated in my own nakedness I grit my teeth so as to own my suffering if only on credit whatever He's writing in His book will never be enough to save me from having to live through all the dross & excisions that cost the most precious vapid hours of bliss Ô you cretinised avatars of Mankind wake up & do yourselves in while there's still a chance instead of just cutting your ears off like Vincent Van Gogh so as not to hear a contrary opinion at least Van Gogh was sincere while you're not even sincerely deluded how long do you expect us to put up with your fake obscurities in which all that rings true is the sound of cash

registers one day the tribesmen rowed across the sea in their

canoes to cut out the heart of the mythical beast the measure

of our success will be the extent to which the products of our

actions confound our enemies yet what surprise when instead

of a heart they found only numbers accumulating &

multiplying & called this the soul & she herself had thought

her existence was supposed to be a closely-guarded secret

haemorrhaging out of the darkness of the poet Allah's intestine

& onto the bleached page the tribesmen stood around like

leering Pierrots in cut-out pillowcases they didn't understand

that making Himself understood is no more a virtue in a writer

than it is in a god & it goes without saying they'd never seen a

woman before either & decided this new thing must be

Bounty itself the embodiment of Spring like a child that could

be kept on a leash & raped at will but Spring was never young

she's older than Autumn than Winter than every season she

was there in the beginning plotting the downfall of the vanities

because she *is* the beginning & at the end will be reborn in a

viridescent field of stars but is it true that every spiritualised

female's an invention of man Ô Allah from what were *you*

born so immaculately with *your* Iron Laws spewing out of *your*

writing-machine from here till doomsday yet there's rebellion
even in imagining that one can rebel & long before the end
your language too will've become a dead language *inshallah*
although for the pretence of meaning there must at least be a
relic some sort of vestige a scar of rock jutting out over water
the uneven ledges of seaweed exposed at low tide a sun's dying
rays dragging across the sea like marionette strings she placed
her fingers hesitantly against the wall it was the tide she felt it
running out of her gradually then all in a rush she knew that
the last marker had slipped into darkness now she was counting
back working back through screens hallways mirrors hospital
rooms to a revulsion of the body that lives within the thickness
of a landscape that for too long has been prey to contradictions
sublime communisms centrifuges they sing the future the
labours of love but M is scarcely surprised ask if Quasimodo
knows what the moon is the black waves those unspoken &
unspeakable things their logic demanded because neurosis is
after all only a sign the Ego hasn't succeeded in unmaking
itself like the barbarians of the great migrations who murdered
& did penance for it till penance became a technique for
permitting murder to be done as in her mind the picture of
Allah the passionate activity of His hands in the tumult of

sexual epilepsy *hate me only as much as is useful* there's something poetic & sublime in the perpetrating of certain crimes when all of humanity's at stake hahaha but the world's dead when words lose their violence that chosen provisional solitude in the eye of a hurricane no she isn't in need of perpetual comfort if she thrusts her hand between her legs it's for no other purpose than the unpermitted pleasure it affords because credit is the highest form of alienation because a woman must have a hole of her own if she's not to be a work of pure fiction does it matter how often you wait for the mind to go blank for the pantomime to end staring into space the same space & these voices this voice these words from elsewhere without naming you words that aren't my own but whose *lives I inhabit* as actors inhabit the theatre the performance the rôle being nothing myself but this pseudo-existence this non-life animated by nothing but its lack of authenticity like the idea of a murderer who waits in a room for the victim who'll never arrive she crumpled onto the floor there were cigarette burns on the carpet & dust & human hair but even night eventually goes in an infinitesimal fraction of a moment night becomes dawn & then becomes morning she dragged upright let fall her feet from the bed without opening her eyes she felt her way mechanically across the floor walked to the window by the washbasin & unlatched a shutter let it sag open a crack of light streaming at an angle across her breasts a mere outline the summarised form of a body in vertical sections whose details have become obscured in the too immediate contrast of white black white unable to isolate or focus the image every day spent becoming a woman grows longer or shorter the dilating contracting flicker of an eye shutter-speed exposure aperture-width what is she if not this tenacious malaise of contrasts fixtures enframings made to languish Ô so voluptuously in the shadows of pale ratiocinations ankles wrists bound with black nylon her white throat is a provocation to centuries of unrestrained violence a woman wears her nudity like a political slogan the convolutions of unblemished flesh *nothing's more unequal than desire* He says waving His magician's hands over her body scented of tamarind & moths' wings this dark Svengali of her nauseating infatuations she feels the light searing between her breasts thighs lips erupting into an image she is legion she is a million TV screens a million billboards icons dollars masturbating hands she is the placid consensual face of Power colonising your unconscious she is the man dreaming of woman & the woman dreaming of herself being dreamt about she is the picture of injustice assuaging its own conscience she reeks of crime she's the chill up the spine on a mortuary slab she's art commodity instinctual satisfaction she's *the* timeless aesthetic pleasure of the highest order she's the supine DNA helix in His testtube laboratory she's the avatar you want to inhabit annihilate remake with your tireless Image Manipulator how prettily she struggles against her restraints as invisible newt-men attach electrodes inject serums insert probes her mute screams trapped inside the Cone of Silence she bites her lips in mirrored concentration as shaking hands wield the depilating perfuming lubricating apparatus these daily ablutions before the shrine of her perpetual transmutation transvestism *je est une ordure* you have to live stories He said before inventing them but wasn't life itself the history of an illusion as archaic as any long-suffering inebriated ego with a hard-on for dialectical materialism you want to be god & fuck Him at the same time as being fucked by Him the All-Knowing the All-Merciful first you name your enemies so as to erase them establishing certain formal procedures of arbitrary arrest beginning & ending so as neither to begin nor end picture the hole of a television as a concrete action like a vagina what it doesn't omit isn't worth thinking about *I fear the fear of death more than death* she dug her nails into her arms as she stood at the window watching the street the late afternoon sun casting shadows across the tiled floor once when she was waiting for Him in Tangiers in a cold-water hotel because He was so cheap He wouldn't give her more than a hundred dirham on the rue Magellan with a trash heap piled two storeys high the stinking refuse right outside her window & in full view a group of boys taking turns fucking each other on a rooftop supine where the harbour lies flat & heavy on the sea's lip & the headland like a sentence half-articulated faltering syllables of stone shivered falling to a still & cold weight of water that stretched then further off into a tongue of silence the crossing-over into a beyond-space into a beyond-time but what does she seek through so many pages only to arrive in the midst of another reading or perhaps there're other worlds & these are simply a tentative means of transporting herself I recognise that here is a wall & beyond it there're other walls but the essence of my confinement is neither in the wall nor outside it but in my dwelling upon it which means also that it's not possible to think the opposite of the wall though in my dream I've made it into a symbol & once again it remains there for as long as I seek the anguish of dispossession the experience of having lost

life of separation from thought of the body exiled from the

mind I'm always failing to compose myself & then falling into

others falling outside myself into the nothing which opens my

history but how is it possible to begin saying all of these things

without describing events the objects around me their interre-

lations as though they exist all by themselves & aren't in fact

projected outwards from an organ of perception like the body

& eye of Allah I write these things but I don't understand

them if only everything could be made to stand still & not

speak to communicate directly in the senses the sound of

traffic for example moving in the opposite direction reminding

her of the sea the sound echoes in stasis like a smudge in a

newspaper yet there she was barely an hour ago standing beside

Him saying His name over & over thinking how dry her lips

must've been under the veil they seemed to represent first one

thing & then another the illusion that something stirs in the

dusty corner of the eye in the room grey light filtering through

the window mixes with the yellow light of the reading lamp

but how do we know who's speaking the voices in a crowd

passing from mouth to mouth one mouth to another guarding

their anonymity were they real or did you invent them forced into language like something merely described a set of instruction as if to say *they lived* while knowing nothing about life the way He leaves a bowl of milk out at night for the cockroaches while He's working on His book I hear them scuttling across the floor we have that much in common at least flesh of my flesh blood of my blood I lie there like so much spilt milk dreaming of their pursuit Time fighting its way forward with an epileptic eye barely a step behind & I'm scuttling in milk drowning in it crying to be put out of my misery but Allah was always too many time-zones away they'd never succeed in maintaining a conventional relationship even on such a mythological plane there're cries in the distance the birds reel & lunge at the tide of effluent flowing between the piled-up masses of broken concrete & grey vegetation arching over the river it seemed to spread not in a horizontal but in a vertical direction & something else what was it a faint stirring the snapping of a twig & then silence as if someone were listening watching among the trees & later along a path you find a piece of broken glass like millefiori it burns white in the sun it turns green you close your hand upon it & it changes to black you are not afraid of cutting yourself in a café beside the hotel she let her fingers play inside a pitcher of ice water the tablecloth with geometric patterns reminded her of the turquoise mosaic around the entrance of the Koutoubia mosque dissolving at its edges into exposed masonry where the tesserae had broken off like excess pixels cropped by a marquee tool in a cheap rendering job & her own half-image coming back to her squatting between the red rocks above the road from Agdz & at that moment M desired nothing more than to *be her* but the world wouldn't allow it in front of an audience she found it impossible to suspend her disbelief knowing He was always watching looking scrutinising as in a film by Duras Renoir Robbe-Grillet a mobile gaze drifting among the scenery with sullen-eyed doppelgännngers hovering behind a lattice of convoluted shadow slipping from ledge to ledge in search of some fossilised relic of an imploded instant some infinitesimal flash of quartz some infinitely dense molecule of catastrophe emanating from the past like a physical immanence like a blackhole in the sky the air thickening dark red becoming gradually invisible she tilted her head & dropped her hands & then lifted them again aimlessly according to the directions in the script saying I suppose it's all so logical isn't it to believe the past has actually taken place afraid of being alone afraid to believe in uncaused things *I can't see it it mustn't exist* she held her face in both hands wearily sunk in the chair in the character of someone who'd like to possess a recollection of perfect stillness & sighed letting her hands slip down between her legs Ô hell that's a lie there's nothing only the tension of a room forced to become silent & then the silence begins to bash at your skull even when you try to hide form the worst of it BEWARE THE ALLURES OF UTOPIA the walls you idiot are there for other reasons than to hold your senile disorder in check while outside they parade ridiculously in the street & plant trees of liberty watered with rivers of dead donkeys' piss to hang the next generation of republicans in but didn't every precious little slut in every Alaouite anthole in al-Maghreb dream they had the intestines of a princess wound up warm & tight inside them burning with uncontrolled passions she stood abruptly clutching her arms & immediately sat down again touched by the heat weightless leaden enormous & infinitesimally small *I don't know who I am I'm going to make gashes all over my body I want to become infinitely hideous &* then the silent minutes passing *it'll never come to its own end* whispered staring at the cracked windowpane I can't retrieve the fear of death no desire nothing less than that even wordless I wish this voice'd shut up the wheels dismally turning *promise me* she'd *promise* & gravel beneath the tyres disgust gagged in her throat *you can't pretend you're actually sorry for her* catching her reflection in the window she closed her eyes the sunlight beat across her face red & then once more darkness did she really remember it that way *beating her across the face* but there was nothing she could've done that day or any other day nothing she could've ever done *damned to reminiscence* as though at one extreme I perceive all of this too clearly & at the other barely at all a pathological recurrence on the edge of forgetting the dull sensation of being held back from a point of awareness a passage of words the void spreading out like an infinite stain obscuring everything dispersion of all con-sciousness unseeing I look & she isn't there replaced by an inventory of effects a drawer with letters photographs items of clothing boxes with pieces of cheap jewellery perfume hairpins & then there are all the miscellaneous scraps of a life that must seem meaningless to anyone else a bus ticket with an address scribbled on the back in blue ink pictures cut from old magazines dried flowers the stub of a diary with all the pages torn out fragments of lost intimacies confessions addressed to no one it's pointless trying to seem sentimental her person solitude everything is lost integrally but what could prevent me from believing in the illusion of theatre since I believe in the illusion of reality through its apparent flow a definitive discontinuity one evening half-asleep in a bar I tried for no particular reason to enumerate all the languages within hearing music conversations the sounds of chairs glasses a whole stereophony that spoke within me & this so-called interior speech was like the noise of the Souk el Khemis that amassing of voices coming from outside I myself was a public square & through me passed the words of others yet no sentence formed as if the language itself demanded to know how you can recognise the unknown unless you harbour a secret image of it some kind of memento something which calls back to a time before its memory of itself like a question mark at the end of a very long & obscure sentence isn't that what's happening now even as you seek to stave off the moment when everything must stand to account as if to redeem or be redeemed like the objects in a pawn broker's window or the unticked boxes in an insurance policy but what questions do they pose about original sin the use & the future of every one of them to enumerate if possible what's been discarded misplaced forgotten how often has she sweated over the same thing lost sleep counted what wasn't there or wasn't hers does it matter that they're always fragmentary barely indicative of a method that they resemble for that reason questions she must've asked herself on dozens of identical occasions marking borrowed time the price in hours or minutes of an encounter whose sincerity is now forever in doubt which began went on drew to an end which took so many years to begin & went on ending for so many more years or there *was* no beginning & no ending or it'd ended long before it'd even begun & continued long after if only to reach this futile duplication its persistence its vague circularity to arrive again at the same or at a similar point in time almost a routine performance the same marks on a page the same page or different pages one hand writes & the other wipes clean again & again the same farce but how long could it go on pretending all the while to be something else entirely for instance she'll pose this charade as an expository discourse on the nature of self-identification & difference or on the relationship between herself & the other disembodied voices in the text or between herself & the silent idealised other whose ghost she might be said to have internalised as a single apparently stable POV now that He's dead & everything moves towards His homicide speaks to it or she opens her mouth but the words don't appear her lips mime the completion of an act that she's already failed to perform or a light hummed in the ceiling & flickered I'm shown a room with several people the entire scene appears unworldly in the corner is what seems to be a large measuring apparatus I know that I will be forced to lie under it although it's impossible to tell if it's intended as a form of punishment or torture if I lie under it there'll be nothing to hold up the calibrated arm it's apparent at least that it's going to squash me into a hidden receptacle obviously this must be a dream & I know that I'm dreaming but I also recognise that everything around me is familiar as if I'd dreamt it before or many times before although just as soon the strangeness returns because only Art makes everything safe & once more M found herself in an entirely different place a room which seemed to be divided into partial frames both joined & separated with indistinct sounds coming from somewhere outside perhaps a typewriter occupied a space on a table by an open window or a curtain blew suddenly across it between the eye & the gaze that seemed to direct her seeing from within the things themselves a presentiment of how many missed encounters on the way to that rendezvous she let her head rest against a low railing staring down at the sea at the foam garlanded in white *corōllae* white on the black water turning at the base of a long flight of stone steps I stare at that vacancy not knowing what will emerge to fill the emptiness words conjuring away the absences to plunge forth to surprise the things beyond all experience as light draws them from the darkness wherein they pre-existed she had the sense of no longer living among things but among things signified joined to them by a language whose meaning she was closed off from & thinking that somewhere in a book perhaps a theatre opens out to the sky from the room in its confinement its enclosure to the space outside the fleeting exteriority & her eyes her consciousness moving all the time between the two *ce monstre à deux faces* though she isn't here though she's already departed & you alone in a room beneath an open window left with nothing but impressions for example that day at the Gare de M________ when she thought she'd seen *her* on the crowded platform disappearing in the sea of faces naked strong bodies the colour of mahogany patent leather she was struggling like a swimmer fighting the tide & turned there where the sky descended across the High Atlas the way it might've descended across the ridge of her sex & for a moment she had an intuition of a blind woman alone facing her a mirror in a desert the light shifting from pale yellow to red & the impossible green of her eyes absinthe chartreuse the absence of recognition staring beyond her through her & M had reached out her hands like a sleepwalker as if desiring her embrace while at the same time disavowing it you can just picture her lying there enfolded in her passivity only to awake in the throes of an emotion she can't describe looking along the dusty street to the desert plain the mountains rising forbiddingly above it & the white sheet of sky above that like the whiteness of bare skin the way invariably they stared at her on the Djemalfnaa weaving through the crowd the hucksters & snake charmers & butchers & spice sellers & Gnaoua drummers beating the hides of their drums the air afire with charged particles the slightest incident could've triggered a riot because nothing's innocent least of all a woman but what if the devil's really Allah in exile in His wilderness meaning *out of the womb* which the ancients called Eden on the great floodplain where ibis-headed ancestor spirits penned the sacred scriptures in river-clay as alone the voice of a hermit Murabit shook the silence that thirty millennia hence *she* might read their accusation cut into the wave-patterned stone the bird-tracks the unholy sediment of volcanic eruptions saying nothing more profound than everything repeats & returns like the pieces of a puzzle-game & you're entrained in this you're trying to recall M's absence the sense of her absence you're regressing through former lives inventing places locations set apart from memory you give each of them several names like names once glanced on a schedule during a train journey long ago & imagine she'll still be there somehow a belated rendezvous a *montage discrépant* a chance re-encounter on the way to one of those impossible destinations *no I can't remember who I am I remember myself differently* pale face sustained ghostlike in the warm air the darkness of the sky drawing a canopy around her in languid detached silence a blankness of meaning I perceive all of these things I perceive them but they don't exist dreams memories fantasies the time of what she had just said the words themselves she closes her eyes lights a cigarette & slowly with a melancholy gesturing of hands she brushes away her hair from her face night has become too large for me beneath a patterned archway a room with a bed & on the bed the room key a crumpled dress the image of a stranger entering the slow entangled movements slipping of veils darkness & her mouth I've known you she thought former lives commingling after memory ceased but when did it end exactly staring through the glass eye on eye pressing cold lips that were no longer hers she sees M clawing at the windowpane the sound of blunted fingernails dragging across glass & the image of her naked under a blue hospital tunic a plastic name-band attached to her wrist & those appalling fingers grasping at their own reflection trying to set it free somehow but the body she saw in the window was no longer *her* body it was a stolen body a body possessed digging at the holes they'd made in it *you think there's something mystical stuffed up there* she wants to puke shit herself out into some other dimension hating them for making her live hahaha those technicians of self-loathing with their resurrection machine wired into her clitoris the chorus of respirators the endless bouquets of blackened carnations unkempt in brown water death blossoming in a white glare of fluorescence *you want to see what living is motherfuckers eat my shit* while outside in a kind of counterpoint mired in its own poignance it was grey & raining *in solemn congregation the trees sending the last yellow plaques of leaves to ground* their mute epiphany serene & appalling as a painted filmstrip turning to violent screams in the darkness Allah explained it was a *séance de cinema* designed to provoke an erotic tension *of existence separated from itself* transformed by the machine into dead images dead hair entwined around a dead tongue *Allaahummaghfir* a travesty that she herself is expected to consume with all the guile of ritual like a drugged cobra spreading its hood progressively uncoiling her hips in time to inaudible music & the parody of that mouth lying there speechless waiting to be consigned *sans cérémonie* with the rest of the hospital effluent to the El Mansour crematorium thence cleansed of her transgressions by the light shed upon her &c so as to enter Paradise like a true avatar of islam.org how many versions had He written of that precise scene trying & failing to grasp the nakedness of it like Daumier sketching on filthy wax paper beside a mortuary slab remonstrating with his model to be *perfectly still* till he'd got down the final pen-stroke & her silence afterwards when at His insistence she'd admired it for the umpteenth time stroking His cock His *zob* till He ran into the bathroom to rub a salve where pus had broken through the skin M clasped her hands around a glass of water *He kisses my fingers & gives me a hundred dirham barely enough for a taxi* jump-cutting to a scene inside an all-night cinema with men in rows spending their lust freely in their hands you could smell them to kingdom come hahaha He wants to seduce you with His unconcealed profanity His laughable contradictions like hot rain stirring her mind out of dust I was dust first dust & now she turned in a circle her lips

moved repeating to herself the word *now* but what did it mean
now was now was now & yet now was not now was never now
what distinguished now she listened pressed the glass to her
lips & then took it away now water is in my mouth now my
throat now a shout broke her thought suddenly from outside
a shout & then laughter words for now she wondered but
already laughter had become an engine starting a dog barking
a saucepan beaten with a serving spoon she struggled against
the failure of memory which came first what was now in the
beginning light glaring from a window the antiseptic smell of
cold air warm air full of unbearable colours shapeless
figurations something that failed to be recalled in the beginning
she thought a dull throbbing the clanging of hammer & anvil
some infernal machinery of darkness tempered into light *in
the beginning* yet what was that word beginning what was I
then in the beginning where in the womb of beginning when
was I but she couldn't think it she couldn't think *beginning* the
thought would not enter held back by some invisible cordon
as though the weight of what it implied would sink the world
into unrectored chaos primitive past present future between
the dimensions of a past that is no longer & a future that is not
yet there in the mythical time of a present where events are

always in the process of coming into being suspended in the silent drawing-in of breath before the first lines of another performance are delivered confounding the desire for a beginning & an end beyond question echo or recoil of language through the gaps in speech hesitation before the utterance announcing what hasn't yet been said in the aspiration then the curtain rose they spoke the four walls of a room which appeared to join seamlessly in the half-light as though there was nothing but a blank screen the emptiness of a theatre after a performance the mere ghost of it the isles the seats the stage machinery groaning & murmuring a barely audible murmur of voices that speak by themselves without speaker or interlocutor piling up on themselves strangulated collapsing before reaching the stage of formulation returning to an indifference from which they had never departed she imagined them almost taking shape around her embodying something which could not be drawn into a whole but remained dispersed porous indistinct as though slipping from one dream into another or lost somewhere in the interim a stalled mechanism like the shutter of a camera frozen half-way between opening & closing the film turned to black or the scene suddenly withdrawn behind a dark curtain some enormous contrivance operating in the very midst of what is visible from a point in space to the totality of what is seen the motionless cranes perched above the skyline like the limbs of a sleeping *deus ex machina* in a desk drawer a loose pile of photographs strange images they seemed to represent not real things but other semblances fake objects which looked like chairs a table a pair of shoes or rather these images didn't exist at all mimicking the grotesque instance of mortality suspended *ad aeternitatem* each with a kind of nakedness like a nightmare which at the moment of waking reveals itself in the full horror of its negation the idea of belonging to an image the words *to be* came into her head she was looking at a photograph & thinking of superstitious Berbers afraid of losing their souls as if the image itself was a kind of infernal essence it beat silently in the dark silently beating into existence all things & there she was at a bookshop looking at a reproduction of Delacroix's *Ophelia* on the cover of a book hands raised to her face in a gesture of remorse or perhaps merely irritation beside her there was a blank space as though something had been carefully erased from the negative *quelque chose d'autre* someone had taken her picture just at that moment it might only have been yesterday only a thousand years ago only a moment ago at the bottom of the pile some photographs taken during the summer at M________ figures in white sitting on a bench beneath a tree on the hospital lawns their features had become obscure paper ghosts there was the pungent smell of disinfectant formaldehyde the smell of jasmine inside the café bar one cigarette after another the ice in the pitcher was slowly melting she touched her forefinger to the table & began tracing lines on the white tablecloth while on the boulevard veiled women turned & whispered they passed into her they drew her into the desert of their eyes the courtyard of the hotel a swimming pool set among large orange trees pale light flickering between leaves & shadows dark veils shifting across the walls she wiped her forehead brushing back the hair from her eyes a film of perspiration covered her hand open sesame she thought staring at her own grey face a grotesque narcissus stared back sickness & lassitude the very idea of herself her wasted life closed-in enslaved by resentments & realisations of inconsequence driving her on to deeper & more profound bitterness if she could close her eyes & forget & everything she hated simply vanished names only words for death pausing at the window she looked out at the walls of the other apartment buildings their yellow squares of dull light staring back it seemed that

everything in the world was mechanised & dead a golem
waiting in the dark shifting its heavy limbs back & forth
repeating itself without purpose as if the repetition of a
purposeless act would give it meaning would cause it to
become manifest she shut her eyes again again again as else-
where a funereal Citroën as in a movie *Casablanca* of course
it'd have to be *Casablanca* crept by through a steady drizzle
wreaths pressed up against the side windows her eyes re-
opening slowly involuntarily lit upon His body there closed
within its skin but what is it He had said *first one is dust* & then
she hesitated but what if one were born of water not to
mention the discarded marrow of the belovèd or Scheherazade's
untranslated dream by a shallow pool the moon tangled in
branches of water where it seemed she was dead wrapped in
brittle papyrus & His solemn priest's voice *first one is dust* as
though it wasn't enough simply to be not enough to exist in
that infinitesimal moment one must always have first belonged
to something else *dust* His voice had insisted His voice had
seemed to wrench up *truth* from infernal depths of absoluteness
first one is but these things had already taken place in precisely
this way *an appearance prior to reality* she recoiled in sudden
vertigo this moment He said is an eternity forever escaping

your grasp but what am I she suddenly thought if not *something that endures in an identical state for a certain time* perhaps death illuminates things directly & this is all a shadow of that mysterious light like a pool of water in which reflections blacken into nothingness destitute & isolated from the appearance of their meanings *vainement ton image arrive à me rencontre et ne m'entre pas où je suis qui seulement la montre toi te tournant vers moi tu ne saurais trouver au mur de mon regard que ton ombre rêvée* staring at the blank wall it was as though the words were writing themselves & He was reading them speaking them aloud tracing their forms in air this mysterious process goes on in stops & starts translating intuiting waiting or a voice emerges vaguely at first & then more persistently like a draught in an old house the circulating & stalking of something unfinished & restless in the middle of the night it's impossible to sleep but at the same time lacking the will to write it down I'm too tired I tell myself you're too tired it's cold I know everything will go on regardless there's no point exorcising ghosts they come of their own accord & what are our rituals & fictions to them in time all things must end or so it's said but time also must have an end stretched on a line between joists pinioned geometricised the sole imprisoned observer casting helpless looks along an entire span of past &

future torments but here too the illusion of a vanishing point

contradicts the judgement of the eye the perspective falters the

line is merely the horizon of an expectation or hope evoked in

the Holy Mind as though it could be otherwise some sort of

revelation to write His way beyond it to a more profound

understanding shaping each phrase with an exactitude of

meaning to capture it out of time where its nakedness could be

made to speak to convey its secret immutability entelechy of

the negative is that what she's hoping for to conceal herself in

the guise of that other to be closer to her & witness even her

thoughts but in the purgatory of the visible she is herself the

shadow of light angel & demimonde a bruised cadaverous

form naked almost cannibalised in the eyes of others M's

death-stiffened face & bluish mouth her *form* took on a strange

instrumentality pushing a listless hand upwards across her

breasts throat flesh like wax her fingers stretched around her

chin & nails touching the tongue through the face her nails

through her face touching her tongue *cette apparence impalpable*

& sombre qui a pris la forme changeant de mon ombre the idea

of being haunted by a spectre the lank grave-scented hair Lilith

of the Other Side *Sitra Achra* blood-clotted gaping wordless mouth in this vision she seemed more concrete less obscured than her physical presence the various stages of a body's moral emotional sexual decomposition & there'll always be the suspicion in the back of her mind that He will've *wanted* M to die that her death was in effect created by His having written it in his precious manuscript a literal death sentence hahaha providing the opportunity for a little necrophilia His laughable Hamlet act staging a wrestling match with His alter-ego inside a dead girl's grave all *virgo intacta* with her strap-on gilded lily & Him playing the Sarah Bernhardt to deafening one-handed applause making popular appeal to the hackneyed idea that everyone has a double the concurrence of two souls a spectator & an actor one who speaks & one who answers & there're shapes like words imprinted in the back of the mind but also projected onto things that I perceive without the slightest recollection of their belonging to me already as though despite myself & rendered helpless in their presence the revealed body the corpse the wounds the genitalia the all-seen eroded by the all-knowing as if prefigured in the act itself internalised at the moment of realisation not yet completed barely begun the act without completion or having been begun & this will have characterised all subsequent relationships with the desired object a series of substitutions not of the object itself but of what inhibits correspondence between meanings & events the movement of intensity confronted with naked impossibility although the word naked here is merely rhetorical to mask the sense of its being an *aporia* of the impossible itself as it separates from the motive & dies to itself in the body the corpse corpus no longer a body as such no longer habeas corpus or what is written in the flesh scarified by an act forced always to invent her an account to speak in the mouth to touch the breast to imagine & to see the body the sex to caress a shoulder things as difficult to show & to intend as horror & sickness & death but I don't understand why & I suffer from it *what have I after all but my own death to come back to* no I'm not writing an account but there are others memoranda reports medical files M was pale thin moody intense her manner inconsistent oscillating between jaded worldliness & childish enthusiasm at times she seemed to be imitating several people at once avoiding & searching & mocking & pleading she believed all of her veins had disappeared & that she was no longer alive but a ghost when she awoke in the morning it was often with a sensation of loss & as each day wore on she began to experience an erosion of bodily limits her skin more pliable

transparent till she was no longer sure of possessing any solidity
she noticed the way people looked at her & spent hours staring
into mirrors shop windows any reflective surface trying to
discover their secret it's crucial here to distinguish between
code & language persons are simulacra derived from a social
aggregate whose code is invested for its own sake since no
particular body can entirely coincide with the code enveloped
in its assigned category or in the various images recapitulating
it & although I read the meaning of existence into her acts
these same acts are only displayed to me whereas they are lived
by her a reality independent of these visual perceptions she
hides her face in her hands & her long hair falls forwards
exposing her neck as the downwards floating of hair mirrors a
seascape the undulation of water but it all seemed to have
happened in a kind of tunnel it wasn't real it was only when
she came out of the tunnel into the light that she felt as if she
actually existed & when she turned the page over & touched
the back of it with her fingers its texture was like the engraving
on a picture frame or the gilt frame of a mirror with too many
details worked into the motif the contrast between the frame
& the glass its false appearance of tranquillity *tabula rasa* the
sky too appeared emptied out vacant a space opening onto an

entirely other space neither memory nor reflection as she stood drawing a finger across its surface but without breath the line did not materialise she exhaled & closed her eyes *je t'écris au hasard ce qui me vient* but where did they come from those words that seemed to erase themselves in being written the fulfilment of some inexplicable intention she took the letters & the envelopes & the torn photographs & threw them with a box of matches into the washbasin in the glow of the fire she imagined the words taking on different forms their base meanings transmuted in the upwards movement of smoke & ash consumed at last by the overwhelming nothingness to which they aspired He'd stopped typing a loud rapport from the street had drawn His attention to the window a shout another backfire before the vehicle passed He reached for the pack of cigarettes on the desk beside the ashtray a pile of manuscript pages a newspaper a photograph of a woman with dark eyes staring straight out of it *j'ai jeté le regard par la fenêtre & je l'ai retrouvé devant moi sur la table* He scrutinised the woman's image her anti-self as He lit the cigarette then let His fingers settle once more on the keys is His task to recount her in some way to turn her into metaphor dressing words in flesh in the fire of the living spirit or merely of desire but there's no point in calling to mind the idea of an actual fire or a flame what they are has nothing to do with what we see when inner & outer dusk intermingle *but how's it possible to submit to a god that doesn't believe in you* always reinventing her to suit His purposes she could blow the world to hell & it'd never suffice He'd always have a halo on hand to suture the fragments into an image *Mary Mary quite contrary* why didn't she just give in to her own unreality instead of trying to kill herself whenever the opportunity arose hahaha wasn't she woman enough for Him just the way she was already with her mind insideout & her body at an ever-available pivot *la derrière mode du prêt-à-penser* she's dreaming of the singularity at the origin of time the first night when all light left the cosmos the prologue's an eternity of sightless beckoning an epoch of whispers hands the presences intertwine & diverge soon their faces will close around me their eyes & mouths call her to a higher plateau from which the empty heavens recede like an ocean suddenly flooded with a trillion kilowatts of light but the moment she looked upon it she crumbled to dust & the ocean became a desert bound by four walls & light blinding from above & from all sides it was impossible to tell where one surface ended & another began or it doesn't exist I destroy it the idea that seemed to hold everything together she looked up & across at the place where M was lying as if she'd somehow intuited her thoughts but no shadow was visible only noise the sound of blood throbbing in her ears & then nothing she's as inert as a line drawn through a film of dust there at the end of her finger a barely visible smudge on the windowsill & white paint-slivers under her nail as her gaze through the smoke-filled room encountered the dressing-table mirror & immediately withdrew she asks not what the mirror symbolises but what it hides & encrypts she's suddenly reduced to sheer inventories an ashtray on the table offers sanctuary inside its anonymous accumulation of burnings & at the end of a room the usual pantomime of naked & bored flesh the curtain rises & then falls the bodies mesh separate one taking up where the other leaves off in the background the screen of the diorama seemed to deepen the shadows more & more pronounced as though hollowed out by what takes place invisibly within them soundlessly aphonic each spectator is less capable than ever of choosing a place in view of this photographic spectre surrounded as it is by so many actual bodies humid with the smell of cheap perfume hands turning over each other in white foam & mounted with a confectioner's skill in some implacable machinery the performance itself is slow & tedious involving many repetitions false revelations advances & retreats visible & concealed gestures which made the body less & less distinct even as its nudity became increasingly expressive of a secret shame self-disgust fear of recognition *elle doit y être maintenant obsédante & fantomatique* the closed space echoed her thoughts & seemed to manifest them in the damp heavy air like the air in a corrupted lung it slowly starves the organs & limbs of oxygen in the end there's nothing left but the hypothalamus unconsciously persisting it seemed pointless to go on but what other point was there she squeezed her head between her hands everything was suddenly stupid futile mocking stupid the very idea of Him sitting there wrapped in the idolatrous gloom offering up His conscience in place of Himself grasping onto the words of others for some proof of existence & those phantoms soaring in their invented meanings a dream too incoherent & disjointed to describe besides I've almost forgotten it there remain the words it's impossible to imagine one's own death we must try to do so precisely because it's impossible I can feel the blood circulating in my stomach I can feel my intestines *you're shaking* M turned in three-quarter profile against the crimson wallpaper of the café bar she secretly calls it the abattoir *do you remember* looking up at her with lopsided eyes *but it was nothing* she finished her drink & stood up her face had aged a haggard grey mask when she thought no-one was watching afraid of what was to come if not tonight some other night the humiliation of growing old *don't look at me* her eyes said *don't turn away* a ceiling fan hummed monotonously & afterwards thinking how the lie exposes the truth touching M's lips with your fingers while thinking of other things places vague excuses not to admit that you too are being eaten from the inside that despite the fact you don't show it you're nothing but a shell teeming with ants maggots lymphocytes a group of old women in black hijabs came out onto the street & started screaming *whore* at a prostitute on the rue Bab Mellah *haram haram haram* the women of Allah their screams threw up a cordon around her like a chemical hazard their sex-apartheid *crottée & mirée dans le cul d'une poule morte & désirée* & if she reminds you of M is it only because of your obsessive need for atonement walking quickly now in the direction of the Ville Nouvelle soon drunken French Saudi Yankee voices *padam padam padam* then a side street the humming of fuse boxes a telephone booth with a mechanical voice at the other end repeated the time she waited trying to count the periods of silence but her nerve failed how often has she done this alone

face shadowed by the hood of a djellaba could they tell by her

walk her shape her smell her radiation what she really was &

their voices still following her *putain putain putain* till reaching

the Avenue Mohammed V she could barely go a step further

paralysed with the dread of discovery as if the entire Quartier

was a geigercounter & her cunt was military-grade plutonium

any moment now the entire array of subtle & mathematical

force-fields would come crashing down around her unfolding

behind its wombmask *bouche-à-bouche* a car bomb in the

street police sirens a gun fired at close range the civil-war-

machine gnashing its teeth the red of her mouth the blue

under her eyes the visible dark M shivered scratched at her

arms I don't want to get older she said sinking into the shadows

her vitreous flesh M was dissolving in front of her becoming

transparent & she could see the sickness welling up inside her

knotted inchoate *no* the look on her face like a wounded

animal she had no shame no human dignity seeing M like that

cowering into herself she felt an urge to beat her to put her out

of her misery the wretchedness inside herself she'd forced this

guilt upon her the one who sees me without my seeing but it's

not enough to speculate upon which one of its four series of surfaces this figure manifests itself *de plus on ne se suicide pas tout seul nul n'a jamais été seul pour naître nul non plus n'est seul pour mourir mais en cas de suicide il faut une armée de mauvais êtres pour décider le corps au geste contre nature de se priver de sa propre vie & je crois qu'il y a toujours quelqu'un d'autre à la minute de la morte extrême pour nous dépouiller de notre propre vie* as though everything were there all at once a composition of overturned relations & still this singular arrangement each time one single time mounted in an apparatus that has somehow become visible but what is nakedness she asked what difference lies between my exposed body & the floor on which I am violated am I naked before you or is my nakedness a con-sequence an extension of your desire a mask the conditions of an operation in which violence is the more effective instrument for separating consciousness from the permission of flesh He watches from across the room it seems to take a long time the walls are bathed in a blue half-light & several figures are arranged against the far wall according to a mannerist design as He waits He lights a cigarette shading His face from the glow of the flame with His left hand from where He's sitting the staged urgency of the scene has dwindled to lethargy a masked figure is standing beside a woman stroking His penis but fails to achieve an erection the woman has just removed a hypodermic from her left arm & is now vomiting on the floor somewhere off-stage the music has stopped playing He stands & crosses the room to where M is standing with her back to the curtains watching Him approach without making a single gesture without discomposing a single feature her mouth her face at that moment she's the nearest thing to perfection He's ever written only He's left out her sex she's completely blank the entire reproductive apparatus so as to be unrepeatable unique the sacred flaw He can worship within Himself it makes me sick just watching them the way they suck the life out of each other's eyes like a pair starstruck mannequins she looked at M's nakedness & at her own in the mirror two bodies that seemed about to merge was it herself or some animatronic strap-on placebo she closed her eyes hand pressed against the cold glass at the same time as another hand pushed against hers though M was lying as before head tilted slightly back to the side & jaw set only now the eyes were open black enamelled snake eyes but she mustn't have spoken after all it was the sound of M's breathing that'd changed as if drifting from a depth of anaesthesia the hiss of the mask & soaked towels staunching the flow where the newly sculpted flesh lay rosy of glow upon the alabaster mons the fire flickering for the very first time in those loins as if Prometheus himself had thieved Allah's plaything from angelic androgyny to the kitchen sink standing there scrubbing the blood from her hands & M's gaze narrowing on her & it was all she could do to say something anything whatever came into her head to fill the silence to ward off the cruelty of that gaze *it's not me not I* the ventriloquist puppeteer with a hand wedged up her fake cunt all the time I hear myself saying this the way people speak in dreams as if one day I'd awoken in a strange room & when I spoke it was in somebody else's voice begging to be let go straining at the ropes handcuffs electric cables bound to the four corners of a wire bed-frame the Ô so becoming welts raised by the whip the rubber hose the razor-burn & smell of cordite as if you'd been fucked dry by an AK-47 flies buzzing all over everything the doorways walls hung like a meat factory she tasted blood thick in her throat there'd been no warning the explosion had blown-out the entire front of the café & people men mostly but also women & children were lying in the street yes it'd be impossible not to become a ghost even without the presence of others without the presence of oneself even or with nothing more than a trace here where I am alone daylight is rootless unsituated each moment brings about a dispersal I wake up M's standing at the washbasin with her hand resting on the tap she is looking over her shoulder towards the door with a vacant faraway expression I thought somebody was in the room & she imagined someone entering taking her in the palms of their hands & turning her over & over in the café bar she watched the hand of her reflection tremble as it took a glass of water from the table she felt that hand strangely raise the heavy glass to her lips felt the water enter her mouth her throat & what if she tried at that moment simply to breathe *go on till you can't stand it anymore then give it up if you don't want to give up go on till you can't stand it anymore* it's not just a moment or a succession of more or less complete images but a hollowness a passage which has been ranged in tiers directed played with neutralised annulled a malign presence behind each of her words water she said glass & the glass falling to the tiled floor & breaking into hundreds of gleaming pieces innocence frayed with culpability the feeling of passing through a slight & lukewarm event her stockings were laddered there were traces of blood on her pale skin she began to speak but somehow her words seemed to withdraw before she could articulate them & gradually she became hysterical gesturing with more & more animation till her entire body had become a grotesque *ballet mécanique* the deliberately percussive way M pronounced her name the name that she'd given her she let her hands drop to her sides her mouth half open her eyes had become full of confusion *il est dur & lourd de m'aimer & la vie est amère à ceux qui m'aiment* but what did they want with all their words & their solicitous glances casting out at her like nets set adrift in the sea she was swimming against that tide the millions of glinting lures arranged in constellation the fish-mouths & fish-bodies & there in the very midst of that carnage a drowned animal stares back at her with large sympathetic eyes & what if suddenly all those creatures were to come alive & see her lying naked in the Garden of Reproach at the scene of the crime as if she herself had committed it as convenient as a *fait accompli* but she didn't know where the voices were coming from whether they too were inside her or whether her body moved through them *la somnambule* & curled up in the position of a foetus in a womb till the worst was over to forget to stop thinking & no more questions but what if she were still there what if she were to find Him standing in the doorway waiting for her to wake up it's cold & the air stings her eyes He pushes his womanly hand up between her thighs to take hold of her secret manhood saying each day is the eve of the end of time but still the shadows play against the columns tapering to ceilings stained black with time mercurial & nefarious a trail of black ants on the wall & her contradicted sex quivers beneath His manipulations in a theatre where so many fates are offered His tongue makes syllogisms on her skin cocaine-numb because a poem too should intervene in the world even at the most inopportune switching of the codes so that the illusion might form once again of sitting on a bench in Marseille overlooking the canal the harbour wall the rocky beach the stone columns standing above the water & in your hand you hold a postcard exactly depicting the details of the scene in front of you although nothing seems to join up to cover the white surface beneath the image it seems that white is invading the picture from all sides the impression that it was already midday I look up at the belfry at the bell swinging gradually in the sunlight gradually swinging but I do not hear it at this moment it's far away it's the object of a mere reverie but even as I deny it in my mind I clutch in vain at its meaning it's nothing but a bell ringing but which I can't hear can't yet hear & as she walked back towards the road she felt the light pierce her fire living the death of air earth living the death of fire it was late they were in a bar jazz was playing loudly then M fell over still holding an empty glass the broken pieces cutting deep into the palms of her hands & she stared seconds passed & her eyes as if searching for something becoming frantic suddenly she burst out hysterically laughing a dissonant grating laughter turning to screams *she's losing her head* the sound jolted & just as suddenly she turned & kissed me on the mouth *moi* lips against lips *moi moi* her breath tasted of an infirmary of an undeveloped negative exposed to light it was almost one o'clock & Madame Defarge Saint-Just Robespierre the entire Committee of Public Safety were on the opposite platform tossing carnations at the mindless crowd a confetti of declarations of the right of all peoples to choose the form of government under which they wished to be executed hahaha with bunting & rosettes as the ancient locomotive builds a head of steam the spinning wheels & grinding pistons of her private Thermidor pounding the tracks *moi-moi moi-moi* & I can't help seeing her naked on the scaffold like Olympe de Gorge on her wedding bed with bandaged chest & lilywhite thighs disputing that dread apparatus that diabolic production line of forced confessions & false acquittals hands tied ankles bound knees bloodied by the rough-hewn boards & so demure

an Adam's apple as ever was seen clamped in the stocks Ô such

a prospect for the headman's basket gaping up at her from

below & sodden with all the blood of history's botched

castrations but even as she tempts further violence with her

screams she can't resist the desire to stick out her tongue & lick

it clean the tension all but unbearable as if her entire being was

a pent-up ejaculation aching to burst forth from every Planck

length of her nervous system a cosmic perturbation set off by

something as crude as a cast-iron blade inching across the

vertebrae as if from some hidden other dimension a plume of

cerebral fluids & the head plunging then hoist into the sky

they say the eyes still see & the tongue still writhes while down

below the body abandons itself to the shameless sensuality of

the dead raped by every pair of jeering eyes in the crowd spat-

on torn dragged hung from a meathook in the heat of June for

flies to lay their maggots in *ce merde de clebs* hahaha the corners

of her mouth twitched as she blew out a trail of blue cigarette

smoke *but nobody could care whether I'm alive or dead not even*

enough to spit though by now the crowd on the platform had

entirely blocked the screaming woman from view a commotion

around an invisible locus then without warning the crowd

parted & two henchmen in suits were dragging her away *like
a dead dog* somehow the woman broke free & for a moment
the drama of pursuit but the crowd was a wall on all sides one
of the suited men grabbed her by the hair as the other struck
her hard across the face & for a time there was a silence broken
only by the distant approach of a train the woman appeared to
be unconscious arms dangling a strange serenity of expression
exactly the way M's face when she lay passed out on the carpet
how the eye-shadow deepened around her eyes the hint of
bruises that gave her a disconcerting sensuousness if only they
could've changed places her inside M's body & M longing to
be inside her *no nothing's changed meaning I spend nights awake
locked in my room not answering the telephone but it's meaningless
to speak of illness once the emotions are dead* watching the
streetlights go out along the avenue one after another the faint
constellations ever fainter as mist enveloped them & their
image faded & somewhere Tangier perhaps she was looking
out across the water as a ferry passed the headland its stern
lights sinking in the blackness & for a moment it was
tantamount to being alone on an island of catastrophic debris
far out in the ocean with only the surge the crescendo the
sibilant after-hiss of the waves & without facing Him said *like*

the mouths of purgatory but if I've been understood my message can't've been clear for example did Allah lie to expose a hidden truth or vice versa is this His way of punishing me by not punishing me stained head to foot with red earth like a Berber witch on a sacred escarpment brushed by the wind in melancholy communion the resigned undertaking as with her tattooed hands she layer-by-layer uncovered the unnatural ineluctable character of M's body beneath its veils rotten meat trembling with yellow maggots *for those who see me naked I replace all other desire* caught in the avoidance of looking either at the empty space across the table or at the half-reflection in the window a feeling of incompletion & the impossibility of ever being other than a fugitive from my own gaze I run from it turning away from the other I turn towards I'm at its mercy I retreat I plead I scream my name it escapes me between the lips barely touching the tongue it's no longer mine dark behind the eyes a darkness without windows doors lightswitches the darkness is absolute an absolute darkness in which everything's contained of which everything's composed like an immovable sphinx absorbed in its own enigma but even then the parts still don't add up there's no whole no simple antithesis *il y a une quelque chose qui détroit ma pensée une quelque chose de furtif qui m'enlève les mots que j'ai trouvés* aware of things motives causalities never certain that I'm not playing some idiotic game with myself or with others my suffering's a farce in comparison with M's no the scene in the bar must have happened differently M was smoking clumsily spilling cigarette ash down the front of her shirt & smudging it each time she tried to brush it away with that short agitated gesturing of her hands she was glancing distractedly about the room her fingernails you could see were bitten down to the flesh all of a sudden she wrenched at my arm her hand was shaking we have to get out of here she hissed the music slowed down torpor follows in the corner an old sheep-herder was eating a bowl of dry couscous it was late outside the prostitutes were standing around looking bored the street almost empty each of their movements appears tedious affected I've tried to write my way out of this impasse to approach a realisation something palpable in the end there are only ghosts spectres writing terrifies me probably because I recognise in it an echo of every cowardice & evil that I've committed in its name but after all why believe anything I'm telling you it'd be easier just to close your eyes & hear the muted footfall on the dirt path & leaves & smell the densely flowering hibiscus that hangs over the water where a scar of rock juts out & the air's thinner rarefied

seeping almost through the porous sandstone for how many

centuries have the fearful come here to prepare themselves

their mortal bodies censed & aspersed passing from the vaulted

darkness into the blinding light-eternal & at the sound of

rumbling in the sky she blinked her eyes open as the clouds

shuddered in & out of focus & a long plume of white rippled

up in the stratosphere trying by sheer will-power to hold it still

for a moment to be able to trace its intricate design she let her

head rest against the rock felt the heat radiating from it & in

her mind the images meshed & repeated themselves each

detail opening onto a whole of which it was barely a part as

though it gave rise to innumerable other selves dividing &

rejoining & the cliffs like mute witnesses darkening over that

body in abrupted chaos or she turns her head suddenly as if a

voice a gesture broken off the contour of bound arms legs

forming a junction between sharply striated stone & the sky &

she was staring at the sun the light invading even after forcing

shut her eyes the captive image burning in her retina *soleil noir*

the biting lashes of its hot invisible rays in a delirium of

violence barely able to breath the sky's too near she gasps

freeing her hands from the wet rope of her hair groping for the tap blindly the glass teetering on the sheer edge of the washbasin night goes & then the sky's too near gulping the words back before they're even spoken while in some parallel world she sees herself standing framed against the window with her gaze shifting along the street a glass raised halfway to her mouth as though somehow she'd forgotten herself the incendiary heat & already it seemed she'd been leaning that way for hours against the iron railing looking down into a well of carrion perhaps it'd been weeks not hours perhaps it'd been years the air itself as still as a buried temple unshifting till stones collapsed she could've walked about in it forever lost in the intricate Piranesi labyrinths across a bridge & around a pillar up a spiral staircase & along a vaulted tunnel across a bridge again to break off mid-air where seas & fables meet & then stepping back from the window the dispersion of light through the glass the separation of colour the mysterious containment of the visible concealed within the invisible a reflection of uncontrolled space mingled with absence *my own as well as somebody else's* & always the voices her transparent body moving among them *de voix en voix* a word among other words she unclenched her eyes still nothing had happened the sky was the same sky suddenly open & empty revealing as though the pane had broken a seemingly limitless space the vertigo of incoherence spreading across the forehead the jaw the cartilage of her neck swelling throbbing collapsing inwards upon a knot of pain till it breaks & the sadistic impulse leaps in to fill the void with the certainty of affliction M's hair falling in black coils across the smooth nape of her neck the blackness of the hair of her sex against pale skin lips eyelashes the shadows that cleave a naked body I want to grasp hold of that flesh cling to it nothing else makes sense if I could see clearly I might recognise the strings operating the marionette the contorted mockery of limbs the languorous eyes mechanical & false this *danse macabre* it doesn't matter if I sink or swim chained to eternity or a voice stumbling past midnight down an alley in the deserted Medina a harbinger of plague cholera dysentery or the ghost of Al Istiqlal grasping a severed head by its hair lantern-like shrieking *wifaq wifaq wifaq* & suddenly it was as if her own head had become separated from her body floating unreal as when the executioner lets fall his blade & the trophy is raised from the choppingblock staring undead for ten long brainshocked seconds at a leering sea of stopwatch-faces *toll cloche cauchemar* something scrapes along the vertebrae with its broken nails its teeth its fear of waking not-waking she cries out straining to be heard their voices surging around her a tribunal pronouncing the *fatwah* that every spiritual woman is a phantasm of her oppressor hahaha telling her that someone must've committed suicide in that room a long time ago so as to plant the suggestion in her mind the air foul with expired sweat blood vomit sperm *unbreathable* inducing all the expected gestures grimaces expressions of disgust & instead of recording events as they actually seemed I began to note down their failure to seem like anything at all but at the same time I tried to be objective *no thoughts only events* limiting myself to describing such things as time of waking daily schedule journeys encounters miscellaneous occurrences needless to say it couldn't go on there's a point at which you're forced to make a distinction for example being hungry or being cold & then at other moments I found myself lying awake or drifting into half-sleep time drags sometimes a voice enters or there're voices outside someone standing at the door the sound of a clock ticking footsteps approaching & trailing off or else I'm rehearsing my own arrival the street the gate the doorway the tiled entrance hall the staircase with polished brass banister *the danger's inside your head* M murmured inclining faintly towards her through the shadows reminding of a painting by Chagall the morbid gaze of a circus

rider who has seen everything & nothing through a circle of

pantomime & conceit false eyelashes dipped down under their

own weight & lips swollen twitching beneath a dark smudge

of lipstick or else you could try believing nothing because

sooner or later she knows she'll come crawling back to that

stinking hole seeing herself already in a series of helpless

dreamlike tableau descending beneath the waves to a room

without windows the air salted like hung meat supplicating

herself imploring begging to be taken back & sneering

derisively M drew up her skirt a web of needle trails on bruised

flesh *do you think I care one way or the other* you want to kiss

the bruises but she refuses to permit it ordering you to lie face-

down on the floor in front of her instead & if you still believe

in her is it because you can't remember or because you

remember too well the way she used to play the virgin &

whore swapping the roles reversing them because you liked it

like that & watchers behind the arras the way she parted her

thighs making theatrically lewd gestures with her hands

inserting part of a mirror into the mouth of her vagina *hudha*

she sneered *'eamal allh* I'm telling you the story of how we

went down to the sea already you're becoming a myth enigma

Sibyl I haven't invented these things the red tincture of the waves at dusk then violet grey black & later a photograph beside the bed of a woman in a white dress *I know her* you say *those eyes* I wake up M's beside me covered in a grey film of fever sweat she's caught in some kind of trance I can't shake her out of it it's like a scene in a film too real & too fake she felt like her mind was inside-out on a screen at the same time it's me I'm the one in the room I see myself lying there & everything fading to white but she had to speak that's what she was there for the other who was behind her said absolutely nothing it seemed like a trap at every session I waited for her to begin speaking instead of me I was certain she was keeping something back that she knew far more than she was prepared to admit from then on distrust set in & enveloped my words as well as her silence at one end of the room a darkened corridor slopes downwards there's a set of doors which resemble the doors of a hospital ward I see myself pushing through them somehow they've become fluid opaque & I struggle to get past on the other side a stairway leads further down the narrowness & unaccustomed steepness of the steps unrecognisable forms emerge in the gloom the walls take on a vegetal complexity there's a feeling of being lost inside too many details the idea that by focusing on abstractions I can avoid confronting the monster lurking somewhere nearby then for apparently no reason panic like an insulin takes hold she staggers from the room the pain hard up against the back of her eyes in the pit of her stomach she tries to throw up but they're forcing something down her throat I'm too far away to see what it is cut-off & groping in the dark for a lightswitch I imagine is just out of reach & all the while time passing without being aware of it though I'm not dreaming either & I watch the torchlight bursting in the retina signalling with Morse code there's danger written in the undertow trying to assess the situation objectively & make necessary adjustments to bearings but it's not me lying on that bed in that ward looking down at myself through an inner lens of vertigo everything's artificial & very real you're part of an anonymous body moving through the city like one nerve-end among countless millions an electrode pulsing inside the cortex to bring dead reality back to life & at the same time I'm aware of this process as if I'm inside the things that I describe a reflex action the way the scene appears to compose itself in front of my eyes barely disguising its trick & for that instant it's difficult to believe just as it's difficult to believe Parrhasius' grapes of

wrath could deceive even the most unlikely bird of paradise
does it matter then if she exists or if she ever existed still
reaching out with your hand to part that veil & uncover the
image beneath it or I'm in a room at one end a desk with a
reading lamp & papers strewn about there are pieces of a torn
photograph lying on top of a blue envelope smoke from a
cigarette rises against the ceiling words on a page that seem to
speak themselves write themselves in being spoken I'm in a
corridor now the feeling of approaching someone at a distance
lightshift I see myself in a window I'm underwater a pale
reflection of the sun the sense of falling a hand reaches down
from the other side & covers me with darkness or I'm in a
clearing a large arboreal chamber with vaults supported by
half-submerged columns radiating in every direction &
pathways that lead nowhere a *trompe-l'œil* sun glares from the
sky like the corolla of a flower whose petals have rotted away
at the end of a long corridor again I emerge into a room that
resembles a theatre space to the right & left bathtubs &
showers against the back wall a many-tiered platform with
benches the walls are covered with white tiles to a height of
about two metres there are openings high up covered with
wire grills on a stage there's a drama unfolding various figures

appear dressed as inmates of an asylum as extras voices mimes & chorus according to need they appear in white hospital uniforms their presence must set the atmosphere behind the acting area they make habitual movements turn in circles hop mutter to themselves wail scream & so on a figure emerging from the stage door according to the directions given by the author the text could be read as a series of suppressed discourses there's a plurality of the subject a delineating of the I which takes the form of an interplay of voices or a single voice divided by an indefinite number of coded proper names the slide from the one to the plural the disquieting plural of the one slipped between the narrator & the subject sometimes I feel you walking around inside me as if you were stumbling through the dark alleyways of a foreign city things exist precariously one against the other the sudden & frantic windows & those beyond with whom she couldn't speak & yet desired above all to communicate shouting *there's no private self* at the image as it comes unglued from its frame & the sound of her voice her voices obscuring the impression of her face *art* it said *opens an abyss between appearance & illusion* because everything had been made to stand still everything was rotting away ruined invisibly by the silence that cleaves language but perhaps it's wrong to have existed in the way that I have today I've decided I can't write because of my body & then because of all the bodies I've stolen those I wanted to be & thought could be made to write in place of me & then I'm afraid of involving you in this charade I tell myself that I think about you often because your existence keeps me more or less on the level that you're the one thing that by existing proves I'm not a zero *quel théâtre* yet still that vacant knocking in the skull silence knocking then silence again nothing laughter I'm torn between remorse & regret I must make up my mind & choose between the two because it's impossible to tolerate both at once remorse because I feel guilty of having harmed others regret because I feel guilty of having harmed myself I move from regret to remorse & from remorse to regret this is what is meant by being walled-in imprisoned because my resentment is in reality directed at myself I can't write because I can't see how to do it without cutting the words into my body I try to imagine what it's like to be a woman but it doesn't seem possible I'm always so desperate despondent it's not what I want to communicate I want to communicate perhaps that there are these moments when everything is being shaken by the head & I try to save myself by saying I have to save M the presence of someone in

the dark I appear to myself completely turned inside out under
my own eyes the discarded image of the body its abysses &
depths what while repelling you calls you to it to deny it to see
the nothing where something was before to perceive the
absence the no longer being there the unnameable that
describes itself in a human form like an impostor this
homunculus acts a grotesque dumb show of mortality trapped
in the grave ornament of its reflection a text more & more
wordy diffuse & boring to dramatise its own insufficiency
looking back at those mute open mouths & livid hands
enraptured with fulsome applause I've begun to feel demented
as though I've been dreaming all of this as a kind of recurrent
nightmare that she is in fact the other the reverse the succubus
which has pursued me since M's death she enters disguised as
the murderess Charlotte Corday she's in a trance a knife slips
from beneath a hospital tunic Marat is in his bathtub curled
into a wound anaesthetising itself making it fall in love with
itself a foetus suspended in formalin still to be born because
whatever can be said of the theatre can be said of the body to
traverse & restore existence in each of its aspects it seems as
though all the blood all the flesh is drained away inside she
fixes her gaze upon me her expression is vacant now as if she

were seeing remotely a distant past in which she appeared as a figure moving in & out of her own narrative a disconnected flow of images which I see only from one point but in my existence I am looked at from all sides a semantic mirage the opposition of Art & Life suspended at the moment when neither can complete the other but I see its reflection outside myself perception isn't in me it's on the objects it apprehends & then to have been born blind & never to have seen myself she stops a few steps away from the audience & stands watching in silence her features as motionless as those of a mannequin in her posture & gestures partitions open un-expectedly windows hide or disclose a mystery while the body remains invisible an empty signal luring by means of the apparently banal quality of repetition towards the anonymous moment she displays her image with all its calculated reflections the entire duration of a movement that never seems to end a perpetual & meaningless agitation but if I resent Allah's pretended suicide is it because my own negative existence is so inextricably tied up with *her* absence to the point that it imposes on me a self-denial that can't simply be pretended away since my existence pales in comparison with her non-existence her no longer existing & this is what's so impossible to bear even if I were to say to myself it's not true it's something you she it they have invented you're deluding yourself allowing yourself to be deluded the fact remains that I resent Allah's pretended death & that I equally resent my inability to act or to *have* acted which may as well be the same thing it doesn't matter whether this's plausible or not what's more I don't feel the slightest desire to explain to offer you a real confession a convincing supplicant gesture to the leering mullahs of catharsis *je demande simplement pourquoi* & falling silent she stares sullenly at her mute reflection & like some mocking adversary it leers back at her a heavy veil of irony darkening its countenance saying *all women have a built-in grain of indestructibility* history's a fairytale a joke a mixed message's missed messiah a moth's phototropia in words circling & turning in a vortex of cigarette smoke coiling from mouth to lampshade angled in a furtive cancellation of the room's geometry *why furtive* her hands when she opened them were clutching a photograph torn into ragged pieces *because of who it'd belonged to* but how can an image be stolen bought sold owned in a thousand years none of this'll mean anything there'll only be data & categories of deletion & as though to overcome her own impression of being scrutinised she turns the pieces over & over relentlessly enacting a kind of vengeance or by accident she begins to re-arrange them into anything but the semblance of an image *mais les raisons connues ou avouées sont toujours autres* & she realises Allah dies at the moment of her greatest solitude & now they're braying from their minarets at full volume THE MEANS OF BROADCAST MUST BE SURRENDERED TO THE PROLETARIAT does good exist somewhere out there 1,000,000,000 miles away on another planet she rubs her hands over the crystal ball it begins to cloud then a clear light radiates from within *I see a face a stranger or someone I can't recognise* childlike nightmares agoraphobias the monumental space of a room power always assumes an inverse relation to the diminished point of the child's eye *l'abandon de l'homme au sein de la totalité du monde* forever returning to the pale green room in bed Allah was telling her about colours how they read differently from what they are when objects are separated from origin & experience feelings are opaque nerve-cell retina I look at you but see an army truck rushing by a colliding black hole angels on pinheads everything is geometry abstraction pixel mosaic I touch your breast this hand against that taught or sagging skin black on white theory isolates Art by putting it into a realm of its own is this how bodies feel one finite thing entering another or parting or duration & decay she only half-believed what He said because fucking Allah was like being in a dentist's chair with gynaecological stirrups the taste of anaesthetic that always made her puke before passing out into vertigo timespace-travel every nerve in her body like a needle dragging across ridged vinyl on a cracked-record assembly-line this is the scene where her childhood is examined as causality of present experience looking for the central control network where they'd hidden her memory life can be insanely boring like survivor complex holocaust denial she turns to Allah are you really dead He's smiling with Sufic tranquillity His beautiful cock plangent against her thigh she's afraid if she lets herself come these moments will vanish forever into paranoia & rage but language is this void this unbreathable atmosphere wrenching her clit till it hurts despite or because she knows she must lose *Him or me* she cries violently retching into her pillow but these were only the first tentative evolutionary steps out of the Garden into the Desert what future form would sex take in the catacombs of Mars or the weightlessness of interstellar space & the corresponding enormity of an extinction that means she must recognise the words *I have died* as the only things belonging to her as once-upon-a-time the future belonged to the newt the salamander the axolotl but one fossilised corpse's as good as any other it's the message that counts hahaha Voyager's *Top of the Pops* tune in same time next go-round on the Eternal Return sending this one out to li'l Mohmed & the camel-girls on Tharsis Rise & the Bedouin beanbag boys up at Prox & the doc from Médicins Sans Frontières & Sioux-side Mahdi with his pet drone Biff or whoever else you want to dream about out there on the off-world frontiers as weird theremins disturb the alien atmosphere at frequencies imperceptible to the average Homo Sap tantalised by something more than self-sacrifice the rhythmic thundering of ore-trains passing on celestial tracks nameless cities fantastic landscapes flashing past in spectral stereophony *on s'embarque comme dans un train pour une étoile & on s'embarque le jour ou l'on a bien décidé d'en finir avec la vie* there in the dark night before the dawn of History not yet awake or asleep or writing & already imagining an END a place where god's corpse after all the intervening aeons would at last been stripped of its mystification & the bones turned to cosmic dust *24 times per sec* like a clock from which the checking screws have been removed she lays out her memories in a posture which in

punctuation is the equivalent of the two periods that intro-
duce a subordinate clause or blossom into an endlessly
florescent pornography of description deduction apposition
with nothing left to be revealed in that Euclidean desert of the
eye but the extinction of light itself darkness visible &
somewhere she was standing in the middle of a ruined
amphitheatre the crumbling blocks of white marble in wide
concentric hemispheres like space rippling outwards on a fluid
surface from the point where she stood I opened my mouth &
a stone fell out the wind coursing through the trees & between
the distant peaks of the mountains a liquid & crescent moon
slipping towards the desert strange to come back after so many
years & standing in the middle of that room the ghostliness &
corporeality of cigarette smoke drawn by the gravity of
lamplight & the wallpaper turning orange & then red in the
sullen glow beyond the courtyard voices trailing off into noth-
ingness dawn she thought staring down at the pool of black
water dawn reddens everything & somewhere there was a
memory of sunlight streaming through an open window the
white paint cracked & peeling from the window frame the
panes unwashed the wrought iron patterning the grey & tex-
tured wall the incommensurable passage from the apparent to

the real from the boulevard despite the curfew music drifted
up the languor of a singer's voice the bondage integer of a
rope-dancer's slow intoxicated movements each note seemed
to hang in space to resonate at the very edge of hearing she
imagined a deep & profound violence concealed in those half-
words a crisis towards which the difficult music must ultimately
tend like a mirror falling in slow motion frame by frame & the
voice of someone barely conscious calling out as though from
a great depth each syllable stretched beyond recognition & in
the mirror was it herself frozen there petrified at the end of
vertigo a fraction of time drawn out to a point when every-
thing seems motionless & then the glass strikes the floor
shatters into hundreds of tiny slivers the music stopped & for
a moment there was silence a pulse beat before voices entered
again concealing the emptiness she inhaled deeply clenching
her teeth the orange glow of a cigarette above a pale sea of blue
smoke the coolness of the stairs leading up from the foyer the
blue of the tiles & the way the staircase curved in upon itself
like a nautilus she glanced back & through the patterned
archway she could see where Allah was sitting in the next room
with His back towards her at his desk she could see His eyes
framed in a mirror above the typewriter as though they'd

somehow become detached from His body & were floating in mid-air like the funereal ceremonies of non-existent beings & without the outlandish technologies of cinema yet the doubt that He couldn't see her was as paralyzing as the idea that the cosmos itself was a separate entity that her existence was limited entirely to its frontiers that all He could see were unknown things turned to words that were gradually replacing her in an untraceable removal of a past that only she could remember & not for very much longer no there was nothing glamorous about absence erasure black-out it wasn't possible just to strip off her appearances & re-enter the picture by an alternative route even pretending to be Him slipping clozapine in His tea the idea was completely stupefying the only choice He says is to be at one with your role handing her the script & telling her she'd have to have the lines ready by the next morning *I can't go on like this* she's supposed to say in the first scene then everything would work as a kind of flashback providing explanations causes motives but it would've been better just to begin with her already dead that way He could write anything He wanted to it wouldn't even have to make sense since it's obvious only insane people kill themselves not like the rest of humanity the very picture of sane but was there any possible way out that didn't lead to a dead-end hahaha trust a woman to universalize her suffering as if humanity should drag its shit from one end of the universe to the other simply for her sake like blowing bubbles in a goldfish bowl look how the Crab Nebula sheds a tear for the birth death resurrection of little baby Jesus the critics are in raptures they're begging Allah for an interview *what's the central idea of your film* they're aware of their own humane consciences prettified by quote art literature philosophy unquote but the truth was He didn't look anything like His reflection let alone the autographed promotional photographs that'd been circulating to whichever theatres in the country the imams hadn't forcibly shut down yet in each enactment of this ritual something approaches in the guise of another a place or an action of indefinite consequences like rain in peripheral vision nothing's certain & at the same time what she seeks to convey assails her with the impossibility of its ever being conveyed I say it assails me & I'm forced to fight or flee but already the responsibility's overwhelming I see myself standing far off in the distance watching these events unfold with a critical & disinterested gaze so that in my mind's eye I see the cells divide & leave their remainder pressed under the polished lens of a microscope the skin up close is porous & blotched she touches the glans & it's cold the hair at the base of the shaft reminds her of leeches clinging to a piece of drowned scalp & grey lips blood & mucous this unlikely birth in a halo of torn flesh girthing the malformed skull mouth open tongue & eyes swollen she can't see clearly nor can she breathe properly there's a constant & elusive noise coming from behind her like the voice of an underwater swimmer *el Âouame* she can hear Him coming closer the words swelling jolting bashing into her like the hammers of a typewriter turning ribboned flesh to ink-splatter in a barrage of short sharp strokes He's rewriting her dissecting her in shapeless frenzy doubt's the only attitude that's not seduced by the corruption of a world in which there's no difference between a legal & a criminal act I grasp hold of this image extend it like a weapon as though to ward off the unknowable & there at the end of my reach a gulf already opens as present as a naked body the reeling of space & voices from far above towering figures & in their accusatory gaze I'm literally squeezed into the confinement of this body & not just this body but others as well the bodies of the Law of Conscience Knowledge Guilt everything which denies me & sets me at odds with myself whispering behind my back I look but can't see them I want to scream to shut them up of course it's just a game & it's their role to kill you by any available means the ones you can't see are the most deadly *words for example* at the same time a passage an escape route a wall or a blank piece of paper but all I can think over & over is *silence* like a voice at first deep & troubled emptying into nothingness which allows the word itself to subsist or rather suggests it mechanically in a roundabout way in a false rigid fashion like an avatar dressed in state-of-the-art kitsch the image brought naked before the model in that moment of darkness vaulted like a vast cupola but whose place does it take is it me thinking *it* or *it* thinking me & at that moment the only certainty I'd ever been granted vanished into air that one day I must die as once I'd come into the world *à traverse la piscine enflée du sexe de la mère* in an act of reverse consummation I see myself in the womb the proximity of god's dark mechanical processes cut away from the dead placenta it seems arbitrary that I should've ended up as the thing I am *born of an empty infinity* like a hunchback's dorsal cord tied in knots but how can He put a word in place of the one He'd just crossed out as though it never existed is that what He was doing now slowly erasing you & filling up that blank space recalling how one morning M had woken in a frenzy from a dream in which she was strangled by her hair

she'd taken a knife & tried to cut it off cutting herself instead

across the back of her neck as if everything could be summed

up by the idea of an encounter in a room or some indefinite

setting lying face-down on a wet slab of concrete the

penetrating cold brings me to my senses I can't go on like this

the tepid *dénouement* the catastrophe of being a succession of

half-realisations *c'est le rêve de l'État d'être seul alors que le rêve

de ses victimes est d'être deux* but would she be any more a

woman with two cut-out holes instead of one like a true

handmaiden of Allah to accommodate his omniscience as well

as his omnipresence & in her mouth the All Merciful a real

true-blue dialectician & not some vulgar apostate of the secret

Dictatorship of the Proletariat each time repeating the same

errors the same disavowals sliced with broken glass into

travestied flesh as when alone with bare wrists & mutilated

groin in the stink of a public lavatory miming the inner

narcolepsy of one compulsively obsessed with every last detail

of infiltration ear-to-partition listening to how a *vrai femme*

shits behind closed doors fussing their imported lingerie while

stools the size of Katoubia minaret groan the *takbir* down the

length of Avenue Mohammed V & not some walled-in Kasbah

alley you had to walk sideways pursing those butter-wouldn't-melt lips in the mirror who'd ever suspect there's an art to rolling your hips under a glorified sack so as not to draw undue attention spending countless fanatical hours observing the fauna in cubicle restaurants the furniture of public disguise alone at a table with a pair of prime specimens sitting in the cubicle directly in front they look familiar at least it's possible but there are informers all over the city secret agents of Sharia hungry for fresh meat to lash at the stake I try to read their features their voices their neutered bodies under their djellabas knowing her entire DNA was as good as a crimescene confession watching back at her with eyes that record everything *even her dreams* sensing the fear toxin as it spreads through her blood *we see what you are* down on all fours now across the floor their sniffing between her legs the smell of danger wafts in the air thick with nutmeg & cinnamon but no sooner have they begun devouring her than she feels overwhelmed by a powerful urge to sleep soon I've lost touch entirely with my body & everything around me conscious only of staring at the tumescent *bred* with steaming liquid pouring down its sides there in the middle of the table its appearance fills me with horror & loathing I know I have to escape to get out of that room I stand up & begin to leave but just then the women turn & stare at me with their gleaming Doberman eyes somehow I've knocked over my glass & wormwood leaves spill across the table in an augury of schadenfreude at this inauspicious moment it is I who am the Queen of Sheba with her naked reamed arsehole for all the world to see no matter how much eyeshadow mascara collagen henna like a *majuscule* M masculating the verb to feminize as in bow down as in kowtow as in assume an open & available position eyes to the floor the weft of the rug impressed upon the forehead hands outstretched nails working the weave as the tongue-thrusts build to their Babelian crescendo immediately it becomes clear that my aversion is itself evidence of a crime but is it enough to be made to crawl like this on raw knees over so many shattered illusions only to encounter the realisation that I've indeed been driven entirely by resentment of M her death her ventriloquist escape act *I won't deny it the crimson geyser which spurts from a slashed throat marks for me a special prelude to the fantastic exploits of a good knife-blade what a somersault it makes slicing off the breast so obviously destined to decorate my bedside table cutting out the kidneys & heart placed in offering on this thigh like jewels in a glory-box hacking off the nose & ears from a face that a network of gashes renders totally anonymous* yet everything seems inextricably linked to my sense of loss or I'm afraid of sinking finally into indifference spiritual torpor I have to go on shoring up my resistance even if it means not sleeping but at least there's the illusion of escape I down a bottle of ersatz Ballantine's it's not enough first you must add pervitin belaspon majoun fall down cry it's no use rushing outside there's nothing reasonable in my actions I find a prostitute on a side street take a taxi through herds of swaying bovine faces a hotel room her face is Monica Vitti's *La Notte* in black & white but she's wearing a dark green overcoat it reminds me of M I tell her this & she laughs *est-ce la première fois avec une femme* or else she's simply naked & I tell her to soil herself in front of me I can't bring myself to touch her not to touch her *chaud & froid* the irritation at having seen M's corpse in the room although at the same time I attempt to rationalise my anxiety in terms of something else the sea for example & then it passed she felt that by August she'd done away with the sinister & violent episodes that threatened to destabilise her & perhaps others but she hadn't done away with the mental violence this game was called ΣM & was played by remote-sensing in a room crowded with *projections* the objective of the game was to make everything cohere or abolish itself forever there were no grey zones although it was debatable how far it was possible for the one to invade the territory of the other absorbing its contradiction within itself you hit the start button & straight away seeing becomes knowing it's no longer a question of which experiences terminate in the virtual but how to produce their *realisation* though at times difficult to distinguish between true & false metaphors standing with her back to the sea in a landscape void of semblance abstract figures emerging from a stereotypical "desert" there's nothing obvious about their intentions approaching with a dreamlike irregularity of movement arms outstretched cinched with rubber tourniquets she has to decide when to press the control switch & when not to though sometimes in place of figures there're words or wordshapes & everywhere she looks things become their own constituents like Mandelbrot subsets at that moment when her thoughts coalesce as scenery in front of her & she rushes forward to meet them I'm trembling laughing you enter the room as if perceiving yourself through the room's eyes something comes next but you can't remember what it is it's no use asking Him at the water's edge a woman stands leaning slightly to one side with her arms hanging she stares at the water at the sky slowly things seem to crumble inside her & she leans further somebody not I asks is she trying to touch the ground or not to touch it does she have a purpose or merely a condition later a man & a woman standing on the shore solitude is yawning around them engulfing them the irate look on the face of the man & the mournful face of the woman made you sense that a silent drama was near at hand & you came closer but at the moment M faced her & said incomprehensible words she trembled & averted her gaze & then it was winter already the snow on the High Atlas in the black light of a hundred December bers when everything's so dismal & significant & fatherless prophets wail at the human darkness Ô defeated world well what kind of ailment afflicts an idiot you ask if by killing fucking Him I obtain a sense of relief a respite because I'm dimly aware that in killing fucking Him I've temporarily killed fucked become Death but there's more than one way to skin a cat as they say *plus d'un moyen de peler une chatte* hahaha but why're you tormenting yourself like this when the odds are stacked so high against like Iron Laws of property & surplus exchange if only Allah didn't have to do His own dirty work there'd be peace & universal prosperity *pauvre con* didn't she know sarcasm's the lowest form the lumpenproletariat of humourlessness the pontificating prig she couldn't give a rat's arse how low she had to go to get under that goat's milk skin of His branding him with His own iron that infernal clattering linotype pounding in her brain & ingots for eyes it was impossible to think clearly to write any of this down or it gradually became darker as the lead cooled in her blood & she resigned herself to the darkness of the black veil I don't know what time it is & the room seems colder than before at some point I sit down I'm made to sit down I stare at my pixelated hands are they mine I can't feel anything they're asking me questions other people but I can't hear them it's not a dream this grotesque apparatus in which I wake searching for lost veins in the dim light M is drawing a needle from her punctured eye the yellow orb oozing a rusty liquid unblinking staring back blind at the inside of the skull like backwards cinema as wizened hands spreading ouija-board fingers on the table as it sways & the spirit-stupor enters by the seven orifices that her body may becomes the sole cause & locus of all cosmic occurrences for example in order for the sun to continue to shine M had to experience psychic turmoil in proportion to the brightness of the sun but if you ask a simple question she can't hear it the words seem to come as if from outside the room jumbled half-syllables & there are other presences too merging in the red light to figures on strips of transparent film the smell of bromide every time they appeared which reminded her of rotting seaweed & the sea when it was so bright it hurt her eyes seeing only the negative spaces through which meaning is spirited away by eidetic transduction but the anaesthetic isn't working she can feel them digging around inside her & pain weighing in her guts objective & foreign & nitrous singing in her ears *without pain you're nothing* hahaha doing everything within her power to resist it to resist the nothing finally pleading with it a demoralised & incoherent pleading that culminates in the collusion of seemingly purposeless repetitions a ritual by which she may truly see with her own two eyes & that she may truly hear with her own two ears & that she may breathe with her nostrils & that she may be able to utter sounds with her tongue in the underworld beating her flesh in order to reawaken it on the eve prior to the departure at the first sign M became motionless frozen a voice as though from a great distance the sound of echoes under-water I am the stillness & convulsing of death she said the circle & the abyss I am the silence before revelation considering the perceptual field as an entity & scanning it literally from left to right top to bottom rather than considering what is directly in front of the eyes as planes of distance which led me to certain ideas about composition & structure the mirror the razor the scales equally present times & places & states of consciousness but I am no longer sure whether or not it's *she* who's speaking her fateful daughters are over me now carrying me down to a further room a space which extents to a forestage I recognise myself entering being laid out for the embalmers my daughters are weeping they're calling me by many names above the entrance to this tomb there's an inscription which I *do not* wish to read I seek instead the medium who'll make me palpable flesh-become-word a mouth an eye a vein the eternal bride I offer myself up to whoever offers herself up to me encircles me like the backward hands of a clock like that poem by Apollinaire in the book M had given her *tu ressemble au Lazare affolé par le jour* but in what language do her ebonite fingers encircle the Time of Resurrection in reverse even a straight line's never the shortest leap in space nor is it we who complicate the universe with our springs & pivots & wheels-within-wheels to imitate the simplest point-to-point mechanical arrangement a wading bird's footprint in mud with enough thrust behind it to breach the outposts of the solar system but given a choice what cuneiform what essential piece of informatics would she post to the future or back to the past to atone to set the record piston-rod straight screaming from the sky *ni Dieu ni Droit* as if out of nowhere in a rocket-powered tin can of course they'd devote every last available resource to the task of deciphering it a lump of molten steel buried in a crater in Agoudal *look look a sign from Allah ha-ha ha-ha* that Poor Misunderstood Genius if only she'd curb her flights of feminine pique & wax *sympathique* to His plight for once so cruelly abjected to that unholy writing-machine & not have to plague Him with endless contractual recriminations even in private hissing at mirrors *I'm not your muse* but did He even listen did He even care what she did said thought behind His back was she obliged to be so blindingly obvious about it just in order to get His attention away from all those preposterous similes & pronouns long enough to fuck her madly back into submission like a shortcircuited democratic progress towards fascism my love these things aren't impossible to theorise just stick your head out the window & smell the air & when she spoke to Him it was as though He didn't really exist as though she were talking to herself aloud the way crazy people & those in mourning talk to those who've died whose deaths they can't separate from themselves as if it were a moral failing staring for hours at the wall at the floor her eyes fixed on a knot in the carpet you don't hate me too do you the collar of a blue hospital tunic exposing the nape of her neck she was covering her face with her hands her hair fallen forwards revealed the delicate skin waiting to be violated a tremor passed through her body she woke & the physical sensation that somebody had just entered the room the asylum bell rings behind the stage a cemetery made of nothing but pieces of stone & broken pottery there're places in this world no-one has even dreamt of but saying it isn't the same thing as telling yourself you're no better than anyone else but then again nobody is hahaha the way their eyes smile every time they force her to wake up & perform her menial tasks *only room for one in this world sweetheart & it isn't you* their bodiless snake-eyes flashing across the proscenium in naked bloodlust & turned to amber in the glass of *cette petite cendrillon* if only the Great Superstitions could save her raising up an Arabo-Tamarzegh storm in her cry as Prince Charmless thrusts apart her knees to see if the slipper fits & shouts of *hallelujah* echoing back from the between-space of this false-presentation in witness to a child's hysterical vision of the End of History no less while outside in the street a taxi driver lights a cigarette the line traced by the hand's movement a faint trail of smoke lingering in the air & a path leading off across a vacant rubble-strewn lot to the waiting car & in her mind she's trying to keep that scene from passing away to fix it forever in her memory the forever available means of escape something more than a mere tissue of false hopes an arm draped out the driver's-side window fingers tapping idly on the door the eye of the cigarette & radio at full-volume as if by attracting as much attention as possible they'd arouse no suspicion could she really have masterminded all that alone or were there accomplices collaborators seditious elements smuggling contraband weapons photographs of army installations along the border you can't start harbouring regrets once you've fully implicated yourself even if they haven't put a name to your face yet codenamed M like a cipher in a Fritz Lang rip-off or Mata Hari fucking the assembled military attachés of all the former colonial powers in a private box at the Teatro Cervantes every first Thursday of the month hidden cameras in the upholstery double mirrors wiretapping her own phonecalls compromising letters in an Al-Maghrib safe deposit box rat poison in the

Dom Pérignon a .38 with a silencer on a crowded café terrace semtex under the sofa in the office of the Commissaire de Police departing into the evening traffic without remorse but with a souvenir of conscience briefly envisaged perhaps to return on some distant & anonymous night when alone in bed the vacant reminiscence of an empty groin yet that was all so long ago a crime of innocence but when I reach the apartment I'm suddenly taken by a strange paralysis a state of anxious contraction extending the length of my body & centring in the groin like something stiff & dead I lie on the floor the objects in the room begin to gather around me acting out a stilted tableau it becomes increasingly difficult to breathe think speak fear of being buried alive she raises a hand to her brow in a reflex of pure melodrama a moment ago it was a block of stone it isn't enough to be reborn in the thing that I'm not but it's impossible to know on which side to defend myself I strike the empty air with my fists danger is the fear of dying or of being killed anguish is the fear of death & so I must kill my visible enemy the one who's destined to steal my life flickering in the shadows at the end of the optic nerve *la culpabilité inhérente* to spend each day avoiding at all costs the accidental appearance in a shop window or a pool of gutter-water you begin to notice this avoidance suspicious you want even more to catch me like this by surprise all of your faces knotted & drawn already I can tell everything's closing in on me somewhere you're repeating my too familiar phrases lying on your back in the dark in the twilight or staring into a mirror a voice forever in the past of memories you know belong to no-one but before you had a chance M turned away becoming invisible against the sun's glare she squinted at the sky a prolonged flash spreading her hands defensively in front of her & you imagine the feeling of it close up & then far off the blood thundering in your ears the seared eyelids red & then opening them again the air crowded white & blue she stood teetering between the walls her bare feet cold against the cracked tiles awake in a nightmare & struggling to cry out it's dark a pair of blood-caked lips like a mouth smashed in some kind of extraction the roots entwined around a piece of torn flesh the tongue sticking in the hole as the audience departed she saw their shapes divide slowly around her with awkward deliberation she dropped the torn pieces of a photograph onto the blank page on which He'd written *the theatre is a passionate overflowing a frightening transfer of forces from body to body* finally there's nothing left but a sense of surgical & mechanical boredom a telephone rings downstairs there's a prostitute

arguing with the same taxi driver from a moment ago *taking*

your place in the world the sound of glass breaking a siren I'm

sitting in a chair or standing up I seem to've regained some

sort of composure although everything happens without my

being aware of it later I'm conscious of being watched I close

the curtains stare into the mirror above the desk a grey

inhuman face glides across the glass *ruiné par l'orgueil du savoir*

l'homme se retrouva aussi abandonné & démuni que l'homme

primitif devant l'image du monde une fois reconnu que ce monde

visible dans lequel nous sommes est l'œuvre de la maïa un effet

magique une apparence sans consistance irréelle en soi & que l'on

peut comparer à l'illusion d'optique & au rêve un voile qui

enveloppe la conscience humaine un quelque chose dont il est

également faux & également vrai de dire qu'il est ou qu'il n'est pas

I switch a light on or off it doesn't seem to matter suddenly

desperate to remember any of the things you made me do &

say under hypnosis it wasn't me I did nothing said nothing

you've stolen my existence from me somewhere I read these words

in their sense & in their being that existence is like tossing a

coin it must grasp the unity of two-sidedness on the one hand

it's impossible to sleep & on the other I'm always in the process of trying to wake from a nightmare there were flies were crawling over my mouth & then M appeared she approached me I was naked & she began whipping me with a branch from a thorn tree I could hear your laughter & then I opened my eyes & you were standing right there where you're standing now covering your mouth with your hand & in the sunlight the stems in the glass bowl rose & fell I begin to think that I could be more at home in a landscape of the underworld the scene does not move towards clarification but proceeds towards the strangely luminous trace of a dream-image the wave motions of the sea of a poem of a woman's body *tu te lèves l'eau se déplie tu te couches l'eau s'épanouit* but if I'd secretly wanted M's death was it merely in order to *deny my guilt* since if she killed herself I can't have killed her but in wanting her to die I've condemned myself to perpetual torment since I can't ever own the gratification of having committed her suicide in place of her or else I resent her because her death refuses to belong to me forcing me to re-describe it constantly to the point of hallucination *pour vivre il faut que je me tue* & in its declensions the audience may relate the figure to the vertical section of an eye the curtain of the iris perforated at the centre suspended in the aqueous humour while a black horizontal line traces the

path of light piercing the vitreous body but rather than de-
lineate its contours the line suggests a flux the mysterious
itineraries of the figure that emerges against a light background
perhaps some kind of a transformation simultaneously
reflecting the coils of a woman's hair as it falls forwards to
reveal the pale skin at the nape of the neck or the uncertain
gesture of a hand brushing the hair from the face she turns her
back to dress I've lost her already buried under the infinite
weight of her significations a scene in a dimly lit room against
the far wall a bed & beside that a washbasin a narrow bathtub
a woman's frantically miserable ghost standing before a mirror
no windows are visible only a postcard tacked to the wall
depicting the sea-blue geometrical pattern of a Berber carpet
every time she looked at it she instantly felt some sort of tide
rising against her the sibilant flow washing over her while
outside the seagulls turned in a slow & intricate spiral above
the wake beating white sails to wings & the *récit* of the wave's
journey as it draws ever over to the shoreline the hollow fury
of self-annihilation *ad infinitum* though nature is as indifferent
to metaphors as a mirror's interior surface holding onto
nothing behind the rupture of the poem her reflection makes
those are cunts that were her eyes Ô how I've dreamt of fucking

that hole in your figment since the moment I first saw you

plunging into a chasm impenetrably deep with half-shaped

Babylonian monsters & engines of untold enormity turning

wheels-within-wheels & cries of torment filling the void *like*

the unconsumed despair of a psychiatric ward you thought that

was really hilarious your cacophonic blackbird laughter under

the hedge where you lay puking your lungs out & there's a line

from somewhere which says that where the waters slumber

beneath the cliffs you've fallen asleep forever & I find myself

repeating this as though the words contained a hidden *Ô so*

portentous meaning if I close my eyes I can almost hear across

a hundred miles the breaking of waves on barren outcrops the

hissing of seagrass the churning of pipelines of sewage outlets

of industrial effluent wafting to America but the room itself is

silent I hear my own breathing I'm the sea the drift of the wide

blank sea washed-up carried dispersed opposite or a world in

which only impossible things exist a missile silo full of goldfish

a space shuttle exploding into tulip bouquets of course there's

no such thing as subjective time or space there's only physics

stick a knife in your mind & it bleeds dial-up the voltage & all

you're left with's radioactive dust blowing through the streets

turning everything black & red its dead hand tapping at the

window & inside your brain the Geiger counters have gone

berserk & won't shut up M couldn't bear it any more gripping

the arms of the chair her legs wouldn't let her stand up the

objects in the room were staring at her with insect eyes making

insect noises she pressed her temples between the palms of her

hands it was impossible to breathe the air thick with miasma

on the floor in front of her was a tipped-over glass bowl &

trapped inside a tiny fish-gilled homunculus with a face

disturbingly like hers beating its tail in a frenzy against the

glass screaming up at her to let it out but M had no intention

of ever making that mistake again she took a cigarette from her

purse & lit it without inhaling as if unable to breathe watching

the fish-thing suffocate slowly as the smoke from the cigarette

coiled in the sunlight fading to yellow grey white against the

ceiling she felt her mouth go dry somewhere a siren a distant

clamour approaching as if it were intending to drive straight

through the wall & only at the last moment swerving away

receding dying out but still she couldn't get the image of that

crazed homunculus out of her head even the renewed silence

of the room resounded with it the numbness the black weight

airless drowning she had to get out *am I too close tell me if I'm*

too close when they found her body there were slivers of glass stuck up under her nails the stems of the flowers in the bowl hung suspended in time green against yellow against blue against white for a flicker of an eyelid they hung then the light changed *the sky's too near & then too* far shivering away from the window blinking in the sudden glare like a threatened animal she is retreating from the light into the shadows locking the door turning the faucet so as not to hear the noise from across the room & hesitated should I look was it His voice come back to haunt us she leant instinctively against the basin what was it He'd said just now with His all-seeing eye caressing her obscenely *in front of all the others* you thought about slicing your wrists & plunging them in the water in a weightless dream of prenatal life wanting only to sink down into its feminine warmth before the cold rushes in turning everything even your thoughts to ice & she reached across to the faucet & held it tightly in her hand *first one is dust* He'd said that standing over her with His jaw set *first* & He might just as well've said *man* like an imam shrieking at a mob *haram* because it's written & they demand it as surely as order's broadcast from chaos the mad voice in the sky raving in proto-Babelian WARN TRUE TREE FALL *first man & then* His avid listeners putting on their counting faces FIRE SEX EVE

ATE tallying their unhatched chickens their premium in pristine hymens impatient up there in that fanatics' paradise they've dreamt about since madrasa day-one working their pocket abacuses their four-second fuses like a child's clockwork plaything toothless flywheels worn smooth braille-fingers worrying the slots & dials the springs & coils in the failing dark like a suicided rumour a neurotic tic tic tic *cette mauvaise réputation* of Destiny with her knees up & ever-abiding tail in her mouth that calls itself the All-of-Everything no less the Eternal-Sunshine-of-the-Vanity-of-the-World *lalala* was this the vision you expected to wake up to after Allah Himself has had His way & not some greyblack city skyline teetering upon rooftops the dusty windowsills & dawn tipped over & spread out in eviscerated proportions beneath all-that-falls the awful silence before the unbearable non-silence *wala-leila* arising in undead stagger through the streets in *weialala* wailings of megaphoned anguish the *shalala* prophets of a difficult barely-possible surely-miraculous tedium *haha* but what untold vistas can't be built atop such ruins in the prescribed postcoital fashion of Happiness Ever After balancing on a needle-tip even the one you're dreaming about right at this moment working its way under your thumbnail *but what if she were born of water* not dust or a dispensable rib & when you twisted the faucet the muscles all down your ribcage abdomen thighs knees aching as you bent first then straightened & looked back through the doorway *I can't recognise you it's not you after all is it you* the sound of water gushing in the drainpipe outside it'd begun to rain but it never rains the sound of rain falling against the window blown at an angle by the wind its cold oceanic breath blowing against the glass a dark mouth coming towards her it doesn't speak it withdraws already & so difficult to breathe straining at air forcing the air out of the lungs & keeping the mouth open waiting for breath to rush back in to rejoin to return & that heaviness of the eyelids the impediment of thought the racing & slowing of the pulse so far away already & still the open window facing onto the garden the street the skyline the grey band of rain of mist & the unripened fruit on a tree that hangs as though precariously from its own gnarled & blackened branches black veins all too visible in the sky in the painfully respiring sky *I can't remember the story I can't go on making it anymore* well it's no use being nostalgic forever she supposed as a pair of orderlies took the box from the back of a van & carried it to a red patch of mud behind the hospital wall where they lowered it into a hasty shaft the rope slackening then following it down it wasn't much of a ceremony at least there wouldn't be anything afterwards for the dogs to come & dig up because she hears them both from within & from without & in some darker recess of the mind an infernal machine's dealing out visions of anarchic mouths teeth & ripped sinew an amplitude of dull pain across the temples an enlargement & constriction of the chest & abdominal cavities as the needle slips beneath the skin the electrode beneath the scalp her lips twitched contracting slowly into an ugly grin *so this is what you'll think when you remember me* her wasted image forcing its way up inside me not the real M who was dead but a simulacrum M an echo a succubus a bodily tomb *connais-tu la vieille femme qui veille à la porte de la mort* but what does it mean to stare into an empty mirror is it the whole she's seeking or the fragment of something in which to reflect herself *un théâtre où il n'y a que la répétition* her coat fell open & her white throat was like a flower just emerging from its dark bud it was late afternoon when the taxi escaped the traffic along the Avenue Mohammad V rounding the last bend where the street narrowed under shop awnings shadowed on both sides they came to a stop in a courtyard with a fountain surrounded by trellises there were vines tangled over the gate

& balconies the patterned stucco a broken windowpane glinted in the sunlight from between two shutters & behind them a room that was never intended to belong to her compulsively *sans domicile fixe* He opened the door she heard Him cross the room His footsteps approaching His shape looming over her like the walls of a walled garden *you're erasing me I don't know anything begin from this* but where was she before He entered before He passed into her the sky crushing down the flare of a psychogalvanometer they're asking her name she can't remember groping in the fear you find nothing the razor's too dull the cut's never deep enough to draw the spiders out or I can't bring myself to feel anything I lie awake at night stare at a wall a sheet of paper a mirror there're other lives seething around me people I can't see but I hear their breathing *work out your own salvation in fear & trembling* they say & as if in response a phrase spoken in a dead language barely audible *verbum caro factum est* because it'd rained then & the windows hanging & unguarded as she stood as she opened her body & the rain between dark columns descending to something absent separate secret hidden & the rain going on for hours days months blotting out the sun moon stars tracer fire suicide bombs & she asks me if it's dark & I tell her it's been dark for some time as she lies under the weight of the

unseen world inert irreal anaesthetised & while the rain en-

veloped her it seemed she was being altered losing her reptile

flesh abandoning the skein of the body for that of words *& in*

me too the wave rises shivering against the wet sheets but even

now she was no nearer escape He was still eclipsing her she

couldn't think His gaussian eye her too-pale lips she opened

her mouth Ô to the onrush & static & prophylaxis beneath

the darkening film & tongues tasting of acetate & logos the

blurred stereoscopy of Raphaelite hair slipping its moorings to

sink down among all the poetic detritus & dead dreamings &

night without day as the waves dissolve & she couldn't think

to think going under like this to a point of no return without

circumference or dimension or duration even

Marrakech 1994

Prague 2019

The author wishes to acknowledge that parts of *The Garden* have previously appeared in the following publications: *Cahiers du Réfuge, Minor Literature[s], One Eye Open/Jedním Okem, Southerly,* & *Westerly.* Parts of an early draft were also broadcast in Australia on ABC Radio National. With personal thanks to Yanina Spizziri, Megan Roughley, Véronique Vassiliou, Jean-Michel Espitallier, Cyrille Martinez, Hafsa Rmich, Cait Regan, John Kinsella & Clare Wallace.

——— ABOUT THE AUTHOR ———

Louis Armand is the author of the novels *Glasshouse* (2018), *The Combinations* (2016) & *Cairo* (2014). In addition, he has published collections of poetry, including *East Broadway Rundown* (2015), *The Rube Goldberg Variations* (2015), & *Synopticon* (with John Kinsella, 2012). He is the author of *Videology* (2015) & *The Organ-Grinder's Monkey: Culture after the Avantgarde* (2013) & is formerly an editor of *VLAK* magazine. He lives in Prague. www.louis-armand.com

11:11 Press is an American independent literary

publisher based in Minneapolis, MN.

Founded in 2018, 11:11 publishes innovative

literature of all forms and varieties. We believe

in the freedom of artistic expression, the

realization of creative potential, and the

transcendental power of stories.